SUNSET PASS

OR

Running the Gauntlet Through Apache Land

CAPTAIN CHARLES KING

1ˢᵗ WORLD
LIBRARY
Literary Society

Sunset Pass

Charles King

© 1st World Library, 2006
PO Box 2211
Fairfield, IA 52556
www.1stworldlibrary.com
First Edition

LCCN: 2007920625

Softcover ISBN: 978-1-4218-3937-0
Hardcover ISBN: 978-1-4218-3837-3
eBook ISBN: 978-1-4218-4037-6

Purchase *"Sunset Pass"*
as a traditional bound book at:
www.1stWorldLibrary.com/purchase.asp?ISBN=978-1-4218-3937-0

1ˢᵗ World Library Literary Society

Giving Back to the World

"If you want to work on the core problem, it's early school literacy."

- James Barksdale, former CEO of Netscape

"No skill is more crucial to the future of a child, or to a democratic and prosperous society, than literacy."

- Los Angeles Times

Literacy... means far more than learning how to read and write... The aim is to transmit... knowledge and promote social participation."

- UNESCO

"Literacy is not a luxury, it is a right and a responsibility. If our world is to meet the challenges of the twenty-first century we must harness the energy and creativity of all our citizens."

- President Bill Clinton

"Parents should be encouraged to read to their children, and teachers should be equipped with all available techniques for teaching literacy, so the varying needs and capacities of individual kids can be taken into account."

- Hugh Mackay

CONTENTS

CHAPTER I

A RASH RESOLVE

"Better take my advice, sir. The road ahead is thick with the Patchies."

"But you have come through all alone, my friend; why should I not go? I have been stationed among the Apaches for the last five years and have fought them all over Arizona. Surely I ought to know how to take care of myself."

"I don't doubt that, captain. It's the kids I'm thinking of. The renegades from the reservation are out in great numbers now and they are supposed to be all down in the Tonto Basin, but I've seen their moccasin tracks everywhere from the Colorado Chiquito across the 'Mogeyone,' and I'm hurrying in to Verde now to give warning and turn the troops this way."

"Well, why didn't they attack you, then, Al?"

The party thus addressed by the familiar diminutive of "Al" paused a moment before reply, an odd smile flitting about his bearded lips. A stronger, firmer type of scout and frontiersman than Al Sieber never sat in saddle in all Arizona in the seventies, and he was a noted character among the officers, soldiers, pioneers, and Apaches. The former respected and trusted him. The last named feared him as they did the Indian devil. He had been in fight after fight with them; had had his share of wounds, but—what the Apaches recoiled from in awe was the fact that he had never met them in the field without laying one at least of their number dead in his tracks. He was a slim-built, broad-shouldered, powerful fellow, with a keen, intelligent face, and eyes that were kindly to all his friends, but kindled at sight of a foe. A broad-brimmed, battered slouch hat was pulled well down over his brows; his flannel shirt and canvas trousers showed hard usage; his pistol belt hung loose and low upon his hips and on each side a revolver swung. His rifle—Arizona fashion—was balanced athwart the pommel of his saddle, and an old Navajo blanket was rolled at the cantle. He wore Tonto leggins and moccasins, and a good-sized pair of Mexican spurs jingled at his heels. He looked—and so did his horse—as though a long, hard ride was behind them, but that they were ready for anything yet.

"It makes a difference, captain—their attacking me or you. I've been alive among 'em so many years that they have grown superstitious. Sometimes I half believe they think I can't be killed. Then, too, I may have slipped through unnoticed, but you—with all this outfit—why! you're sure to be spotted, followed, and possibly ambushed in Sunset Pass. It's the worst place along the route."

Captain Gwynne looked anxiously about him a moment. He was a hard-headed, obstinate fellow, and he hated to give up. Two months ago his wife had died, leaving to his care two dear little ones—a boy of nine and a girl of six. He soon determined to take them East to his home in far Pennsylvania. There was no Southern Pacific or any other Arizona railway in those days. Officers and their families who wanted to go East had to turn their faces westward, take a four or five days' "buckboard" ride across the dusty deserts to the Colorado River, camp there perhaps a week before "Captain Jack Mellon" came backing or sideways down the shallow stream with his old "Cocopah." Then they sculled or ground their way over the sand bars down to Fort Yuma, a devious and monotonous trip; then were transferred to "lighten" or else, on the same old Cocopah, were floated out into the head of the Gulf of California and there hoisted aboard the screw steamers of the Ocean line— either the Newbern or the Montana, and soon went plunging down the gulf, often very sea-sick, yet able to get up and look about when their ship poked in at some strange old Mexican town, La Paz or Guaymas, and finally, turning Cape St. Lucas, away they would steam up the coast to San Francisco, which they would reach after a two weeks' sea voyage and then, hey for the Central Pacific, Cape Horn, the Sierras, Ogden, and the tramp to the Union Pacific and, at last, home in the distant east, all after a journey of five or six weeks and an expense of months of the poor officer's pay.

Now Captain Gwynne was what we called a "close" man. He could not bear the idea of spending something like a thousand dollars in taking himself, little Ned and Nellie, and their devoted old nurse, Irish Kate, by that long and expensive route. He had two fine horses and a capital family wagon, covered. He had a couple of stout mules and a good baggage wagon. Jim, his old driver, would go along to take care of "the Concord," as the family cart was termed. Manuelito, a swarthy Mexican, would drive the mules; the captain would ride his own pet saddle horse, Gregg, and a discharged soldier, whom he hired for the purpose, would ride McIntosh, the other charger. All were well armed. Parties were going unmolested over the Sunset Pass route every month. Why should not he?

The officers at Prescott shook their heads and endeavored to dissuade him, but the more they argued the more determined was he. There were tearful eyes among the ladies at Prescott barracks, where Mrs. Gwynne had been dearly loved, when they bade good-by to the children. But one fine day away went "the outfit;" stopped that night at Camp

Verde, deep down in the valley; started again early in the morning, despite the protestations of the garrison, and that evening were camping among the beautiful pine woods high up on the Mogollon range. Sieber's pronunciation of the name—"Mogeyone"—will give you a fair idea of what it is really like.

And now, three days out on the Mesa, Ned and Nellie, in silence, but with beating hearts, were listening to this conversation between their father and the famous scout, and hoping, poor little mites, that their father would be advised and turn back until met by cavalry from Verde; yet so loyal to him, so trustful to him, that neither to one another nor to Kate would they say a word.

"Well, Sieber, I've argued this thing out with all Prescott and Verde," said the captain at last. "I've sworn I wouldn't turn back, and so, by jinks, I'm going ahead. It's all open country around Snow Lake, and I can keep on the alert when we reach the Pass."

"You know your business best, I suppose, captain, but—" and Sieber stopped abruptly and gazed through the open windows of the Concord at the two little forms huddled together, with such white faces, on the back seat.

"Well, won't you at least wait and camp here a day or so? I'll go down by way of Wales Arnold's and get him to send up a couple of men. That won't be going back, and you'll be tolerably safe here. The cavalry won't be long getting out this way."

"And meantime having my beasts eating barley by the bucketful so that I won't have enough to get through? No, Al, I've made calculations just how many days it will take me to get over to Wingate, and delay would swamp me. I don't mean to discredit your story, of course, but everybody, even at Verde, said the renegades were all down by Tonto

Creek, and I cannot believe they would be out here to the northeast. I'm going ahead."

"Well, Captain Gwynne, I give up. If you're bound to go there's no use talking. Stop one moment though!" He spurred his broncho close to the window, and thrusting in his wiry arm drew little Nell close to him, bent and kissed tenderly her bonny face.

"God guard you, baby," he murmured, as finally he set her down. "Adios, Ned, my lad," and he shook the little man heartily by the hand. "Good luck all! Now I must gallop to make up time." He turned quickly away and went "loping" down the trail, but his gauntlet was drawn across his eyes two or three times before he disappeared from view. Two white little faces gazed wistfully after him and then into each other's eyes. Irish Kate muttered a blessing on the gallant fellow's head. "Come on, Jim," said the captain, with darkening face, and presently the little train was again in motion, winding over the range that, once passed, brings them in view of Snow Lake with the gloomy, jagged rocks bounding the horizon far beyond. There is a deep cleft that one sees in that barrier just as he emerges from the pine woods along the ridge, and that distant cleft is Sunset Pass.

Though seldom traveled, the mountain road from Fort Verde over to Fort Wingate was almost always in fair condition. Rains were very few and did little damage, and so at a rapid, jingling trot the wagons lunged ahead while the captain and Pike, the retired trooper, rode easily alongside or made occasional scouts to the front.

Knowing that his children must have heard his talk with Sieber, the captain soon dropped back opposite the open window and thrust in his hand for the little ones to shake.

"You're not afraid to go ahead, Ned, my boy! I knew I could count on you," said he heartily. "And Nell can hardly be afraid with you and her old dragoon dad to guard her. Isn't it so, pet?"

And the wan little face smiled back to prove Nellie's confidence in father, while Ned stoutly answered:

"I'm never afraid to go anywhere you want me to go, father. And then I haven't had a chance to try my rifle yet."

The boy held up to view a dainty little Ballard target gun—a toy of a thing—but something of which he was evidently very proud.

"And then we've got good old Pike, papa—and Kate here—I'm sure she could fight," piped up little Nell, but there was no assent to this proposition from the lips of poor Kate. All along she had opposed the journey, and was filled with dread whenever it was spoken of. Vainly had she implored the officers and ladies at Prescott to prohibit the captain from making so rash an attempt. Nothing would avail. As ill-luck would have it the lieutenant colonel recently gazetted to the infantry regiment stationed in Northern Arizona had just come safely through from Wingate with exactly such an "outfit," but without such guards, and Captain Gwynne declared that what man had done man could do. There were plenty of people who would have taken her off the captain's hands, but nothing would induce the faithful creature to leave the motherless "childer." She loved them both—and if they were to go through danger she would go with them. All the same she stood sturdily out in her resentment toward the captain and would not answer now. Jim, too, on the driver's seat, was gloomily silent. Manuelito with the mules in rear had listened to Sieber's warning with undisguised dismay. Only Pike—ex-corporal of the captain's troop—rode unconcernedly ahead. What cared he for Apaches? He had fought them time and again.

Nevertheless when Captain Gwynne came cantering out to

the front and joined his old non-commissioned officer, it was with some surprise that he listened to Pike's salutation.

"May I say a word to the captain?"

"Certainly, Pike; say on."

"I was watching Manuelito, sir, while the captain was talking with Sieber. Them greasers are a bad lot, sir—one and all. There isn't one of 'em I'd trust as far as I could sling a bull by the tail. That Manuelito is just stampeded by what he's heard, and while he dare not whirl about and go now, I warn the captain to have an eye on the mules to-night. He'll skip back for the Verde with only one of them rather than try Sunset Pass to-morrow."

"Why! confound it, Pike, that fellow has been in my service five years and never failed me yet."

"True enough, sir; but the captain never took him campaigning. They do very well around camp, sir, but they'd rather face the gates of purgatory than try their luck among the Tontos. I believe one Apache could lick a dozen of 'em."

The captain turned slowly back, and took a good look at the Mexican as he sat on his high spring seat, and occasionally encouraged his team with endearing epithets, or, as in the manner of the tribe, scored them with wildest blasphemy. Ordinarily Manuelito was wont to show his white teeth, and touch the broad, silver-edged brim of his sombrero, when "el capitan" reined back to see how he was getting along. To-day there was a sullen scowl for the first moment, and then, as though suddenly recollecting himself, the dark-skinned fellow gave a ghastly sort of grin—and the captain felt certain that Pike's idea was right. The question was simply how to circumvent him.

At sunset the little party was cosily camped on the edge of Snow Lake—a placid little sheet far up among the mountains. The plateau was broken by a low ridge a few miles east, through a gap in which, known as Jarvis Pass, ran the road to Sunset Pass beyond. Horses and mules, securely tethered, were grazing close at hand. The two wagons were drawn in near the little camp-fire. The children were having a jolly game of hide and seek and stretching their legs after the long day's ride in the wagon. Kate was stowing away the supper dishes. Manuelito was stretched upon the turf, his keen, eager eyes following every motion of his captain, even though his teeth held firmly the little paper tobacco holder he called his "papelito." Out on the open ground beyond the little bunch of trees Pike could be seen, carbine in hand, scouting the prairie-like surface and keeping guard against surprise. The sun went down. Twilight hovered over them; Kate had cuddled her beloved "childer" into their beds in the wagon and the captain had come around to kiss them good-night. Manuelito still sprawled near the tiny blaze, smoking and watching, and at last, as the bulky form of the Irish nurse-maid disappeared within the canvas walls of the wagon, the Mexican sprang from his recumbent position, turned, and with quick, stealthy step sped away through the clumps of trees to where the animals were placidly browsing. He bent his lithe body double, even though he knew that at this moment the captain and the ex-corporal were over at the east end of their little camp-ground, chatting together in low tones. He laughed to himself as he reached his mules and found them heavily hoppled with iron chains.

"As if I would take a burro when one stroke gives me a *caballo grande*," he muttered, and pushed still further out to where the four horses were "lariated" near the timber. A word to "Gregg" whom he had often cared for; a gleam of his knife from the sheath and the gallant horse was free to follow him. Still in silence and stealth he led him back toward the camp-fire where the saddles were piled. Still he marked that Captain Gwynne and Pike were in earnest talk down at the other end of the camp. Warily he reached forward to grasp the captain's saddle, when a low exclamation was heard from that officer himself and, peering at him through the trees, the Mexican could see that he was eagerly pointing westward and calling Pike to his side. Instinctively Manuelito glanced over his shoulder and saw a sight that told him horse-thieving would not save his tawny hide; that told him their retreat was cut off, and their only hope now was in standing together. Back among the pines through which they had come; well upon the ridge, and not ten miles away, blazed an Indian signal fire. It was the Apache summons for a quick "gathering of the clans."

Now God help the bairnies in the wagon!

CHAPTER II

MANUELITO'S TREACHERY

All this time Darkey Jim had been sleeping soundly, wrapped in his blankets, with his feet to the fire. There was never an hour, day or night, when this lively African could not loll at full length, in sunshine or shade, and forget his cares, if cares he ever had, in less than three minutes. In this case, despite Sieber's warning, which he had overheard, he simply took note of the fact that the captain and Corporal Pike were looking after things and that was enough for him. There was no use in worrying when "Marsa Gwin" was on guard, and within an hour from the time he had had his substantial supper, Jim was snoring melodiously, with his head buried in his arms.

Manuelito was thoroughly aware of this trait of his "stable-mate," else he had not dared to bring the captain's horse so close to the fire. Now his fierce, half Indian face seemed full of perplexity and dread. The Apache signal fire still glowed among the black pines away to the westward. The captain and Corporal Pike were hurriedly coming towards him through the stunted trees,—yet here he stood with "Gregg," all irresolute, all fearful what to do. Back towards those black pines and the long reach of road beyond he dare not go. The Tontos held the line of retreat. Here in camp he hardly dare remain for the keen cut in "Gregg's" side line showed plainly that the knife had been used, and left him accused of treachery. Out of the fire light and back to the grazing ground he must get the horse at once—but what then? Noiselessly turning, he led Gregg, wondering, back to the glade in which the other horses were tethered, and quickly drove his picket pin and put him on the half lariat. But how was he to conceal the severed side line? Off it came, both nervous hands working rapidly, and then when he had about determined to cut off the lines of one of Jim's mules and so throw suspicion on him, his African mate, he was aware of his captain striding through the trees toward him. He could almost have run away. But the next words re-assured him.

"That you, Manuelito?" challenged Captain Gwynne in low, hoarse tones. "All right! Take the side lines off Gregg and saddle him for me at once. I have work to do."

The Mexican could hardly believe in his escape. For the time being, at least, he stood safe. It would be easy enough later to "lose" the telltale side line in the waters of the lake. Manuelito cursed his folly in having used the knife at all. Haste prompted that piece of bad judgment. He could have unbuckled them just as well. But all the same he blessed his lucky stars for this respite. In three minutes he had "Gregg" saddled and ready by the little camp-fire. There stood the captain and Pike in low and earnest conversation.

"I shall only go out a short four miles," said the former, "but I must satisfy myself as to whether those beggars are coming this way to-night. Gregg and I have 'stalked' them many a time and the country is all flat and open for six miles back."

"I wish the captain would stay here and let me go," pleaded Pike.

"No! I'm never satisfied without seeing for myself. You and Manuelito will have your arms in constant readiness, and watch for me as I come back. There's no moon—no light—

but so much the better for my purpose. Is he all ready, Manuelito? Let me glance at my little ones in the ambulance before I start."

Who can say with what love and yearning the father bent over those little faces as he peered in upon them? The flickering light of the camp-fire threw an occasional glimmer over them—just enough to enable him to see at times the contour yet hardly to reveal the features of "his babies." He dare not kiss for fear of waking them. "God bless and guard you, darlings," was the choking prayer that fell from his lips. Then, vigorous and determined, he sprang into saddle.

"Now, Pike," he muttered, "you've been with me in many a night bivouac and you know your orders. They never attack at night unless they know they have an absolutely sure thing, and they haven't—with you three. Jim, there, can fight like a tiger whenever there is need. Watch the horses. I'll be back in an hour or there'll be reason for my staying."

Three minutes more and they heard the rhythmic beat of "Gregg's" hoofs out on the open plateau and dying away westward, sturdy, measured, steady in the trot the captain preferred to any other gait. Pike moved out to the edge of the timber, where he could hear the last of it—a big anxiety welling up in his heart and a world of responsibility with it; but he clutched his carbine the more firmly and gave a backward glance, his face softening as his eyes fell upon the wagon where little Ned and Nell lay sleeping, and darkening with menace and suspicion as he took one swift look at Manuelito, cowering there over the fire.

"Blast that monkey-hearted greaser!" he muttered. "I believe he would knife the whole party just to get the horses and slip away. I'll keep my ears open to the west—but I'll have my eyes on you."

Once out at his chosen station, Pike found himself in a position where he could "cover" three important objects. Here, close at his right hand, between him and the lake, the horses and mules were browsing peacefully and as utterly undisturbed as though there were not an Apache within a thousand miles. To his rear, about fifty yards, were the two wagons, the little camp-fire and flitting restlessly about it the slouching form of Manuelito. In front of him, close at hand, nothing but a dark level of open prairie; then a stretch of impenetrable blackness; then, far away towards the western horizon, that black, piney ridge, stretching from north to south across the trail they had come along that day; and right there among the pines—Pike judged it to be several miles south of the road—there still glared and flamed that red beacon that his long service in Arizona told him could mean to the Apaches only one thing—"Close in!" —and well he knew that with the coming morn all the renegades within range would be gathered along their path, and that if they got through Sunset Pass without a fight it would be a miracle.

The night was still as the grave; the skies cloudless and studded with stars. One of these came shooting earthward just after he took his post, and seemed to plunge into vacancy and be lost in its own combustion over towards Jarvis Pass behind him. This gave him opportunity to glance backward again, and there was Manuelito still cowering over the fire. Then once more he turned to the west, watching, listening.

Many a year had old Pike served with the standards of the cavalry. All through the great civil war he had born manful, if humble part, but with his fifth enlistment stripe on his dress coat, a round thousand dollars of savings and a discharge that said under the head of "Character," "A brave, reliable and trustworthy man," the old corporal had chosen to add to his savings by taking his chances with Captain Gwynne, hoping to reach Santa Fe and thence the Kansas

Pacific to St. Louis, to betterment of his pocket and to the service of one, at least, of his former troop commanders. No coward was Pike, but he had visions of a far-away home his coming would bless, where a loved sister's children would gather about his knee and hear his stories of battle and adventure, and where his dollars would enable him to give comforts and comfits, toys and "taffee" to her little ones. Was he not conscious that her eldest boy must be now fourteen, named for him, Martin Pike, and a young American all through? It must be confessed that as the ex-corporal stood there at his night post under the stars he half regretted that he had embarked on this risky enterprise.

"If it were anybody else now but old Gwynne," he muttered to himself, "things wouldn't be so mixed, but he never did have any horse sense and now has run us into this scrape— and it's a bad one or I'm no judge."

Then he glanced over his shoulder again. Manuelito was shuffling about the fire apparently doing nothing. Presently the ex-corporal saw the Mexican saunter up to the wagons and Pike took several strides through the timber watching before he said a word; yet, with the instinct of the old soldier, he brought his carbine to full cock. Somehow or other he "could not tolerate that greaser."

But the suspected greaser seemed to content himself with a cursory examination of the forage and baggage wagon and presently came slouching back to the fire again. He had some scrap of harness in his hand and Pike longed to know what, but it was too far from his post of observation. He decided to remain where he was. He must listen for the captain. All the same he kept vigilant watch of Manuelito's movements and ere long, when the fire brightened up a bit, he made out that the "greaser" was fumbling over nothing else than a side line. Now what did that mean?

Pike took a turn through the little herd of "stock," bending down and feeling the side line of each horse and mule. All were secure and in perfect order. The one in Manuelito's hands, therefore, was probably "Gregg's," or an extra "pair" that he had in his wagon. There was nothing out of the way about that after all, so Pike resumed his watch towards the west, where still the Apache beacon was burning.

It must have been half after ten o'clock. Manuelito had slunk down by the fire, and not a sound was to be heard except Jim's musical snore, and a little cropping noise among the horses. Yet Pike's quick ear caught, far out on the prairie to the west, the sound of hoofs coming towards him.

"When those Apaches named a horse 'click-click' they must have struck one that interfered," he muttered. "Now that's old Gregg coming in, I'll bet my boots, and there's not a click about his tread. 'Course there might be on rock, instead of this soft earth. The captain's back sooner than I supposed he'd come. What's up?"

Quickly, crouchingly, he hurried forward some few rods, then knelt so that he might see the coming horseman against the sky. Then challenged sharp and low:

"Who comes there!"

"Captain Gwynne," was the quick answer.

"That you, Pike? By jove, man! I've come back in a hurry. Are the horses all right? I want to push right on to the Pass to-night."

"Horses all right, captain. What's the matter back there?"

"I didn't venture too far, but I went far enough to learn by my night glass and my ears that those scoundrels were having a war-dance. Now the chances are they'll keep it up all night until they gather in all the renegades in the neighborhood. Then come after us. This is no place to make a fight. It's all open here. But the road is good all the way to Sunset, and once there I know a nook among the rocks where we can stow our whole outfit—where there are 'tanks' of fresh water in abundance and where we can stand them off until the cavalry get out from Verde. Sieber said he'd have them humming on our trail at once. Tanner and Canker and Lieutenant Ray are there with their troops and you can bet high we won't have long to wait. It's the one thing to do. Rouse up Jim and Manuelito while I give 'Gregg' a rest. Poor old boy," he said, as he noted his favorite's heaving flanks. "He has had a hard run for it and more than his share of work this day."

In ten minutes Black Jim, roused by vigorous kicks, was silently but briskly hitching in his team, Manuelito silently but suddenly buckling the harness about his mules. Irish Kate, aroused by the clatter, had poked her head from underneath the canvas to inquire what was the matter, and, at a few words from the captain, had shrunk in again, stricken with fear, but obeying implicitly.

"Let the children sleep as long as possible, Kate," were Gwynne's orders. "The jolting will wake them too soon, I fear, but we've got to push ahead to Sunset Pass at once. There are Indians ten miles behind us."

A few minutes more and all was ready for flight.

"Now, Pike, ride ahead and keep sharp lookout for the road. I'll jump up here beside Jim and drive, keeping right on your trail. Old 'Gregg' will tow along behind the wagon. He is too tired to carry any one else this day—and you— Manuelito, hark ye, keep right behind 'Gregg.' Don't fall back ten yards. I want you right here with us, and if anything goes wrong with your team, or you cannot keep up, shout and we'll wait for you. Now, then, Pike, forward!"

An hour later in its prescribed order this little convoy had wound its way through Jarvis Pass and was trotting rapidly over the hard but smooth roadway towards the high Sunset range. The little ones had been aroused by the swaying and jolting and were sitting up now—silent and full of nameless fears, yet striving to be brave and soldierly when papa threw back some cheery word to them over his shoulders. Never once did he relax his grasp on the reins or his keen watch for Pike's dim, shadowy form piloting them along the winding trail. Little Ned had got his "Ballard" and wanted to load, but his father laughed him out of the idea.

"The Tontos were ten miles behind us, Ned, my boy, when we left Snow Lake, and are farther away now. These mountain Apaches in northern Arizona have no horses, you know, and have to travel afoot. Not a rod will they journey at night if they can help themselves—the lazy beggars!"

And so the poor father, realizing at last the fruits of his obstinacy, strove to reassure his children and his dependants. Little Nell was too young to fully appreciate their peril, and soon fell asleep with her curly head pillowed on Kate's broad lap. Ned, too, valiant little man, soon succumbed and, still grasping his Ballard, fell sound asleep. In darkness and silence the little convoy sped swiftly along, and at last, far in the "wee sma' hours," Pike hailed:

"Here we are, right in the Pass, captain! Now can you find that point where we turn off the road to get into the rock corral?"

"Take the lines, Jim; I'll jump out and prospect. I used to know it well enough."

Down the road the captain went stumbling afoot. Everything was rock, bowlder and darkness now. The early morning wind was sighing through the pines up the mountain side at the south. All else was silence.

Presently they heard him hail:

"Come on! Here we are!"

Jim touched up his wearied team and soon, under the captain's guidance, was bumping up a little side trail. A hundred yards off the road they halted and Gwynne called back into the darkness:

"How's Manuelito getting on, Pike?"

No answer.

The captain stepped back a few yards and listened. Not a sound of hoof or wheel.

"Pike!" he called. "Where are you?"

No answer at all.

"Quick, Jim, give me the lantern," he called, and in a moment the glimmering light went bounding down the rocky trail, back to the road.

And there the two soldiers met—Pike trotting up rapidly from the west, the captain swinging his lantern in the Pass.

"Where's Manuelito?" was the fierce demand.

"Gone, sir. Gone and taken the mules with him. The wagon's back there four hundred yards up the road."

"My God! Pike. Give me your horse quick. You stay and guard my babies."

CHAPTER III

ON THE ALERT

Obedient to the captain's order, Pike had dismounted and given him the horse, but it was with a sense of almost sickening dread that he saw him ride away into darkness.

"Take care of the babies," indeed! The old trooper would shed his heart's blood in their defence, but what would that avail against a gang of howling Apaches? It could only defer the moment of their capture and then—what would be the fate of those poor little ones and of honest old Kate? Jim, of course, would do his best, but there remained now only the two men to defend the captain's children and their nurse against a swarm of bloodthirsty Tontos who were surely on their trail. There was no telling at what moment their hideous war-cry might wake the echoes of the lonely Pass.

With all his loyalty, Pike was almost ready to blame his employer and old commander for riding off in pursuit of the Mexican. It was so dark that no trail could be seen. He could not know in which direction Manuelito had fled. It was indeed a blind chase, and yet the captain had trotted confidently back past the deserted wagon as though he really believed he could speedily overtake and recapture the stolen mules. Pike thought that the captain should stay with his children and let him go in pursuit or rather search, but every one who knew Gwynne knew how self-confident he was and how much higher he held his own opinion than that of anybody else. "It is his confounded bull-headedness that has got us into this scrape," thought poor Pike, for the twentieth time, but the soldier in him came to the fore and demanded action—action.

Knowing the habits of the Apaches it was his hope that they would not follow in pursuit until broad daylight and that it would be noon before they could reach the Pass. By that time, with or without the mules, Captain Gwynne would certainly be back. Meanwhile his first duty seemed to be to get the provisions from the wagon up to the little fastness among the great bowlders where the children, guarded by poor, trembling but devoted Kate, were now placidly sleeping—worn out with the fatigue of their jolting ride from Snow Lake. She kept Black Jim with a loaded rifle close by the side of the family wagon and prevented his falling asleep at his post, in genuine darkey fashion, by insisting on his talking with her in low tones. She kept fretting and worrying about the absence of the captain and the non-arrival of Manuelito with his wagon. She asked Jim a hundred questions as to the cause of the delay, but he could give no explanation. It was with joy inexpressible, therefore, that she heard Pike's well-known voice hailing them in cheery tones. He wanted Jim.

"Where's the captain and the wagon?" demanded Kate in loud whisper.

"Up the road a piece," answered Pike in the most off-hand way imaginable. "We'll have it here presently but Jim'll have to help. We've lost a linch-pin in the dark. Come along, Jim."

"Shure you're not going to take Jim away and leave me alone with the poor children. Oh, corporal, for the love of the blessed saints don't do that!"

"Sho! Kate. We won't be any distance away and there ain't an Indian within ten miles. They wouldn't dare come prowling around at night. Here, you take Jim's gun and blow the top of the head off the first Apache that shows up. We'll be back in five minutes. How are the kids—sleeping?" "Sleeping soundly, God be praised, and never draming of the awful peril we're in."

"Peril be blowed!" answered Pike stoutly. "We're safer here than we could be anywhere east of the Verde and as soon as it's good and light and the horses are rested, we'll be off for the Colorado Chiquito and leave the Tontos miles behind. Take things easy, old girl, and don't worry. Come along, Jim."

And so away they went through the inky darkness, plunging along the rocky and winding path by which they had brought the ambulance up the steep. Not until they had got down into the road itself did Pike give his negro comrade an idea of what had happened. Then, speaking low and seizing the other's arm, he began:

"Jim, old boy, we've got to pull together to-night. There's nothing the matter with the wagon—that's all right, but that whelp Manuelito has run off with the mules and the captain's put out after him. It'll be daylight soon and he'll get the son of a gun—sure, and then hurry back to join us; but the wagon lies just where I think you and I can start it down the road and fetch it nearer camp. Then we can rake out what provisions we want in case we have to stand a siege. See?"

Black Jim's eyes nearly popped from their sockets. He had been on scouts with his master, and bragged prodigiously around garrison about how they fought Tontos down along the Black Mesa and in the infested "Basin."

To hear Jim talk one would fancy he had killed at least half a dozen Indians in hand to hand encounters. Indeed he had behaved with self-possession and a very fair degree of coolness in the two affairs which Gwynne's troop had had when Jim happened to be along. But this was different. Then they had forty or fifty veteran soldiers. Here—only old Pike and himself were left to defend the position—and no one might say how many Apaches might come along. Besides it was still dark (and Napoleon said all men were cowards in the dark), though far in the east a grayish pallor was creeping up from the horizon. Who could blame poor Jim if his knees shook and his teeth chattered a little, but he went manfully along by Pike's side and soon they reached the abandoned wagon.

As luck would have it, Manuelito had stopped where the road began a pretty sharp descent and Pike felt sure that if they could only start the thing they could run the wagon almost opposite their hiding place. Then it would be far easier to get the stores up the rocks. Taking the pole himself and telling him to "put his shoulder to the wheel" Pike sung out a cheery "Heave!" and, slowly at first, then more rapidly, the vehicle with its precious freight came thundering down the rocky and almost unused road. Pike had to hold back with all his might and to shout for Jim to join him, but between them they managed to control the speed of the bulky runaway and to guide it safely to a point not far from their little camp. The old trooper rummaged about until he found the lantern hanging under the seat. This he quickly lighted, and then, loading a sack of barley for the horse on Jim's shoulders, and lugging a box of hard bread under one arm and of bacon under the other, he led the way up among the rocks until they reached Kate's "field hotel," as he called it. There they dumped their load under the ambulance. Pike whispered a jovial "Go to sleep, old girl. You're all safe" to the still trembling Irish woman, then down they went for another load. This time they came laden with a wonderful assortment. Coffee, sugar, condensed milk, canned corned beef, potted ham, canned corn and tomatoes, some flour and yeast powders, a skillet or two, the coffee pot, some cups, dishes, etc., and these, too, were placed close to the ambulance, to Kate's entire mystification; and then, sending Jim down for another little load, Pike set to work to build a tiny fire far back in a cleft in the rocks.

"We'll all be glad of a cup of coffee now," he said to himself, "and so will the captain; he should be brought back before day. We may have no chance for cooking after the sun is up. Thank God, there's water in plenty here in these hollows."

Out in the Arizona mountains one may journey day after day in July or August, and all through the fall and winter, and cross gulley, gorge, ravine, canon and water cross and find them all dry as a bone—not a drop of water running. It is useless to dig below the surface, as one could do in sandy soil and find water, for it is all rock. Indeed it would be impossible to dig; nothing short of blasting would make an excavation. But a kind Providence has decreed that the scout or traveler should not be left to die of thirst. Here and there in the low ground or in the ravines are deep hollows, in which the water has gathered during the rainy season, and this is almost always palatable and sweet. One only has to know where these "tanks" are, and he is all right. Both Captain Gwynne and Pike had twice been over to the Pass before, and, spending a day or more there scouting the neighborhood, had noted the little nook among the great bowlders and the abundant supply of water. It was God's mercy that this was the case.

And now as he boiled his coffee in the little niche whence no betraying gleam from his fire could shoot out across the gorge, Pike gave himself over to a calm look at the situation. If the captain recovered the mules and got back by sunrise— despite fatigue they could give them and the horses a good feed of barley and then push for the Colorado Chiquito, some twenty miles away. Once across that stream they were comparatively safe, for the Apaches had a superstitious feeling against venturing beyond. That country was considered as belonging to the Maqui Pueblo Indians, of whom the wild Tontos stood a little in dread. Then, a little further on, began the Navajo country, and the Navajos—once the most fearless and intractable of mountain tribes—were now all gathered in at their reservations about old Fort Defiance,—the richest Indians in sheep, cattle and "stock" on the face of the globe. No Apache dare venture on their territory, and white men, on the contrary, were safe there. "If we can only get away before those scoundrelly Tontos get after us," said Pike to himself. "Even if the captain doesn't get the mules, we can abandon the wagon and the heavy luggage, cram the ambulance with provisions and make a run for it to Sunset crossing. I wonder which way that blackguard of a greaser did go. He would hardly dare go back the way he came with every chance of running slap into the Tontos. He has taken hard tack and bacon enough to keep him alive several days. It's my belief he means to hide somewhere about Jarvis Pass until he sees the Indians following our trail and then, when they are fairly past, to make a run for the Verde. The cowardly hound!"

Then Jim came stumbling up the path with his load and the lantern. Pike gave him a big tin mug of steaming coffee and a couple of "hard tack." Took another down to Kate, whom he pacified by saying that the captain was with Manuelito and the mules and bidding her to lie down and get a little sleep before day. Then he went back to Jim.

"Now young man," said he, "I want you to listen carefully to what I say. You had a nap last evening—a sound sleep in fact and I've not had a wink. If I can get an hour or an hour and a half it will fetch me out all right for the day's work. This coffee will freshen you up and keep you awake. You stand guard until sunrise—until the sun is well up, in fact, then call me. Keep your ears wide open; listen for every sound; if it's the captain coming back you'll hear the hoof beats down there on the road; if it's Apaches you won't hear anything. But you take my word for it, Jim, they won't attempt to follow beyond Snow Lake to-night. They can't be here before noon, and by that time we'll be miles away towards the river. Don't get stampeded. Just keep cool; watch and listen. If Kate asks anything more about the captain tell her he's down by the wagon. It was too heavy to fetch up here. I don't want to make a man lie, but we mustn't let her and those poor little kids know he's away. Now are you game for it, Jim?"

The negro mechanically took the rifle that Pike handed to him. "I'll do my best, corporal," he said.

"That's a trump! Now I believe I can rest easy," answered Pike, and so saying he unrolled his blankets, spread them on the ground close by the ambulance, looked to the chamber of his revolver to see that every cartridge was all right, lay his rifle by the wheel, lay down and rolled himself into his soldier bedding, and was asleep in three minutes.

How long afterwards it was that he was aroused Pike could not begin to guess. It seemed to him that he had not slept five minutes yet he had had a good, long, refreshing nap, and now it was broad daylight. The sun was shining brightly and Black Jim was bending over him; his finger on his lips. Pike sat up and rubbed his eyes. The first question he longed to ask was: "Has the captain got back?" but Jim pointed to the ambulance and, listening, the old trooper heard childish voices, soft and low; their bubbling laughter telling of their utter ignorance of the dread anxiety which hovered over the camp. Kate, worn out, was evidently still asleep and the children were chatting blithely together but taking care not to disturb their kind old nurse. Little Ned poked his hand out through the narrow space between the curtain and the frame of the door and peeped through with one merry blue eye as he shook hands with Pike, who had scrambled to his feet.

"Where's papa?" he whispered.

"He's all right, little man," answered Pike, smiling cheerfully up at the bright boy face, though the old soldier's heart was heavy as lead. "He's all right. He's down looking after the mules with Manuelito. You and Nellie hungry? I'll get you some breakfast presently, but better let old Kate sleep as long as she can."

"I'd like to come out, corporal, and look around," whispered Ned.

"Wait a little while, my lad. It's very early and the air is pretty keen. I'll let you out presently. See if you can find papa's field glasses in there anywhere. I want to take a look at the road with them."

Ned withdrew his little brown fist and could be heard groping around the dark interior. The captain had so arranged the seats in his "family wagon" that they could be turned and flattened against the sides of the vehicle, leaving a clear space in which there was abundant room for Kate and the children to lie at full length and sleep in comfort, and this was their tent and sleeping apartment. The captain and his party slept as we always used to sleep when scouting in the dry season in Arizona, without shelter of any kind, in the open air.

Presently the little fellow re-appeared at the aperture.

"Here it is, Pike," he whispered. "But you'll have to open the door to get it out."

Pike turned the handle, took the "binocular," gave Ned a jovial nod and another shake of the hand, closed the door and strode away signalling Jim to follow him. When they were out of earshot of the ambulance he turned:

"Have you heard nothing—no hoof beats?"

"Not a thing," answered Jim. "We can't see the wagon from here, but I could hear anything if anything had come."

Pike looked wistfully back up the Pass. In one or two places the road was visible from their lookout, winding and twisting around the rocks.

Three hundred yards away it turned around the foot of a hill and from that point was utterly lost to view. Pike looked at the sun, then at his old silver watch. "After seven o'clock, by jove! and not back yet," he muttered. "It's full time we were off for the Chiquito, but we can't stir without the captain." Then he turned once more to Jim. "Water the horses and give them a good measure of barley each, then put some dry wood on those embers in the niche there—be sure and make no smoke—and cook some breakfast for us all. I've got to go up to that point yonder. From there I can see all over the open country to the west, and the road, too, as far as Jarvis Pass. These glasses will show every moving object to me, and I haven't a doubt I'll see the captain somewhere out there in the distance coming back to join us. Darn the mules! I don't much care whether he gets them or not, but I'd like about two minutes' private interview with that blasted greaser."

So saying, Pike got a pail of water from the "tank," liberally soused his head, face and neck in the clear, cold water; then, throwing his rifle over his shoulder, the brave fellow went springing down the winding trail to the roadway and then strode westward up the Pass. A few moments brought him to the base of the little hill, a short, sharp climb brought him to its crest, and there, kneeling, he adjusted the glasses, and for a long, long minute swept the open country and the winding road lying before him in the bright sunshine. He could see every inch of the way to Jarvis Pass, and when at last he lowered the glass he groaned aloud:

"My God! My

God! There's not a living soul in sight."

CHAPTER IV

ON THE WATCH

For fully half an hour poor old Pike remained there at his post of observation, every now and then vainly scanning the plateau through his field glass. Meantime he was talking over the situation to himself. "The jig is up now. I've got to go back to camp presently. I'll have to tell them the captain is still away and that I have no idea where he has gone. I might just as well make a clean breast of it and admit that Manuelito has deserted and gone off with the mules, and that the old man (for by this half-endearing appellative the soldiers often spoke of their captain) is in pursuit. I don't suppose he found their trail until broad daylight anyhow." Then he looked back towards the nook in which his precious charges were doubtless impatiently awaiting his return. He could just see the top of the ambulance over the ledge of rock that hid it from the road. "Jim is just giving them his breakfast about this time," he went on with his self-communion. "They could not eat another mouthful if I were to go back now with my bad news. Better wait until they've had a square meal before I tell them. They can bear it better then."

Still the stout-hearted veteran would not give up hope. Again he swept the road with his glass, searching wistfully for some little dust cloud or other sign of coming horseman across the wide, open plateau, but all was silence and desolation, and, at last, feeling that he must go back to camp and get something to eat, he shouldered his rifle and went down the hill, his heart heavy as lead.

Of course it was still possible for him to hitch up the team and make a run for it, with Kate and the children, for Sunset Crossing, but he felt confident that neither Kate nor little Ned would listen to such a project if it involved leaving the captain behind. There was yet a chance of his old commander's returning in time. Although he was not to be seen anywhere over the twenty-mile stretch towards Jarvis Pass it was all the more probable that he might have found Manuelito's trail leading into the mountains north or south of the gorge in which they were now hiding. The Mexican had long been employed in the pack train and had been up through this range towards Chevelon Fork—he had heard him say so. Very probably, therefore, he had struck out for the old "short cut" back to the Verde. It was impracticable for wagons but easy enough for mules—and it lay, so Pike judged, ten or fifteen miles south of the Pass. The very thing! It would be the most natural course for him to follow since the signal fire west of Snow Lake had showed them the evening previous that the Indians were on their trail. Doubtless the captain had reasoned it out on the same line and ridden southward along the western base of the range until he had overtaken his treacherous employe. A huge shoulder of the mountain shut off the view in that direction, but the theory seemed so probable to Pike that his spirits began to rise again as he struck the road Why! It might readily be that at this moment the captain was not more than a mile or two away, and hurrying back, fast as the mules would let him, to join the loved ones whom he had left at camp.

"It's a theory worth banking on for an hour or two at least," said Pike to himself. "By Jinks! I'll swear to it as long as it can possibly hold good. There's no use in letting them worry their hearts out—those poor little kids. God be with us and help me to bring them safely through!" And so, much comforted in spirit, the old trooper—half New England Puritan, half wild frontiersman—strode briskly down the road, determined that he would make no move for the Colorado until he knew from the evidence of his own eyes that the Apaches were coming in pursuit.

The shortest way from Jarvis Pass to the point where they now lay resting, was by way of the road along which they had come the night before, on both sides of which, as has been said, the country lay comparatively clear and open for miles to both north and south. Pike felt certain that with the aid of his glass he could see the Indians almost as soon as they got out upon the plain and while still many a long mile away. Then there would be abundant time to bundle their supplies into the ambulance, run it back to the road, stow Kate and the children safely in the interior and whip up for "the Chiquito," leaving their pursuers far behind. What a mercy it is, thought Pike, that these Tontos have no horses! The captain, too, he argued, even if he had not started before, would have an eye on that road wherever he was, and would gallop for camp the moment he saw the distant signs of the coming foe.

Even as he trudged along, whistling loudly now by way of conveying an idea of jollity to the anxious little party at the ambulance, Pike's keen eyes were scanning the mountain sides. North of the Pass the ground did not begin to rise to any extent until fully half a mile away, but southward the ascent began almost at the roadside and was so steep as to be in places almost precipitous. A thick growth of scrub oak, cedar and juniper covered the mountain and here and there a tall tree shot up like some leafy giant among its humbler neighbors; and, standing boldly out on the very point where the heights turned southward, was a vertical ledge of solid rock. Pike stopped instantly. "Now that's a watch-tower as is a watch-tower!" he exclaimed. "I'll scramble up and have a look from there before I do another thing." So saying he left the road and pushing his way among the stunted trees and over rocks and bowlders he soon began a moderately steep climb. Long accustomed to mountain scouting, the craft of the old Indian fighter was manifest in his every movement. He carefully avoided bending or breaking the merest twig among the branches, and in stepping he never set foot on turf or soft earth, but skipped from rock to rock, wherever possible, so as to leave no "sign" behind him. It was more a matter of habit than because he believed it necessary to conceal his trail from the Indians in this case. No human being on earth can follow an enemy, like an Apache; a bent twig, a flattened bit of sod, even a tiny impression in the loose sand or rocky surface will catch his eye in an instant, and tell him volumes. Pike knew well that there was no such thing as hiding the trail of his party, and thinking of them he stopped to take breath and look down. Their little fastness was hidden from him by the trees, but he could see the baggage wagon down in the road, and, being unwilling to have Kate and the little ones worrying about his long continued absence, he set up a loud and cheery shout.

"Hullo—o—o Jim!"

Jim's voice came back on the instant. "What d'you want?"

"Just save a little breakfast for the captain and me, will you? We'll be hungry as wolves when we get in."

"Is papa there?" piped up little Ned in his childish treble.

"No—he's down around the west side. He'll be in presently. I look for him every minute. He's all right, Ned."

"Where you at?" shouted Jim again in his southern vernacular.

"Up here on the hill. I'm going a piece farther to look at a big rock. I'll be down in ten or twenty minutes."

And so having cheered and re-assured them, Pike pushed on again. A few minutes' sharp climbing brought him to the base of the ledge which proved to be far bigger and higher than he had supposed, and all the better for his purpose. Clambering to the top he could hardly repress a shout of exultation. Not only had he now a commanding view of all the plateau over to the ridge through which wound Jarvis Pass, but he could even see over beyond towards Snow Lake, while northward for several miles the western foothills of the range were open to his view. It was by long odds the best lookout he could have found and he only regretted that his view southward was still shut off. Adjusting his binocular he again gazed long and carefully over all the plain and especially along the western edge of the range to the north, but the search was fruitless as before. Not a living, moving object was in sight.

Finding an easy descent on the side farthest from camp and opposite that on which he had clambered to the top Pike half slid, half swung himself to the base again, and there he came upon a sight that filled his soul with joy. From base to summit the ledge was probably fifty feet in height and was so far tilted over on the western side as to have an overhang of at least fifteen. More than this, there was a great cleft near the base and an excavation or hollow running inwards and downwards, perhaps fifteen feet more. Pike went in to explore, and, to his farther satisfaction, found a "tank" where the water had gathered from the melting snows and in the rainy season. He tasted it and found it cool and fresh, and then, sprawling at full length, he drank eagerly.

"What a find!" he almost shouted, with glee. "We can store Kate and the children back in there, throw up a little barrier of rock at the front with loopholes for our rifles. Not a bullet or arrow can reach us from any direction except the tops of those trees yonder, and God help the Tonto that tries to climb 'em. And, even if the captain don't come, by Jinks! we can stand off all the Apaches in Arizona. It won't be more than three days before Al Sieber will be galloping out with a swarm of the old boys at his back, and if Jim and I, in such a fort as this, can't lick Es-Kirninzin and his whole gang, call me a 'dough boy!'"

The more he explored, the better was Pike pleased with the situation, and in five minutes he had made up his mind what to do. The little nook in which the party had been hiding was all very well for the night and a good refuge for the horses as well as the human beings, but in broad daylight the Indians would have no difficulty in finding and surrounding it, and there was hardly any space within its rocky walls which would be safe from bullet or arrow when once the assailants got up the hillside. Here, however, they could stand a siege with almost perfect safety. From above or from the flanks the Indians could not reach them at all, and if they attacked from the front—up hill—nothing but a simultaneous and preconcerted rush of the whole band could succeed, and Pike knew the Apache well enough to feel secure against that possibility.

Now it was possible to wait for the captain indefinitely. If he got back in abundant time for them to load up and push out for the Colorado Chiquito before the Indians reached the Pass—well and good. If he did not—well, thought Pike, from here I can see the scoundrels when they are still miles away, and all we've got to do is stock this cave with blankets, provisions and ammunition, build our breastwork and let 'em come. "With Kate and the kids out of harm's way, back in that hole, I wouldn't ask anything better than to have those whelps of Tontos trail us up here and then attempt to rout us out. We'd make some of 'em sick Indians; wouldn't we, old girl?" wound up the ex-corporal apostrophizing his Henry rifle.

Greatly elated over his discovery, Pike went scrambling down the rocky hillside in the direction of camp. He no longer took any precautions about concealing his "trail." He well knew that in the two or three trips it would take to bring their stores and then Kate and the children up to the cave, such "signs" would be left that the Apaches could follow without the faintest hesitation.

Five minutes brought him into the midst of his charges, and here for a moment the stout-hearted soldier was well nigh unmanned. Instantly he was besieged with eager and anxious inquiry about papa, and poor little Nellie, who had come running eagerly forward when she heard his cheery voice, looked wistfully beyond him in search of her father, and seeing at last that Pike had come alone, she clasped her little arms about his knees and, looking imploringly up in his face, burst into tears and begged him, amid her sobs, to say why papa did not come. Bending down, he raised her in his strong arms and hugged her tight to his heart.

"Don't cry, little sweetheart," he plead. "Don't worry, pet. Papa isn't far away. He's coming soon and I've got such a beautiful playhouse for you and Ned and Kate up there on the hill. We won't go up just now, for we all want to be here to give papa his breakfast when he comes in. And my! how hungry I am, Nellie! Won't you give old Pike some coffee now, and some bacon and *frijoles*?"

Nellie, like a little woman, strove to dry her tears and minister to the wants of her staunch old friend, the corporal. Ned manfully repressed his own anxiety and helped to comfort his little sister, but Kate retired behind the ambulance and wept copiously. She knew that something must be wrong. No mere matter of a mule astray would keep the captain from "the childer" all this long while. Black Jim had set the coffee pot and skillet again on the coals and in a few moments had a breakfast piping hot, all ready for the present camp commander who, meantime, slung aside his slouch hat and neck-handkerchief, rolled up his sleeves and was giving himself a plentiful sluicing of cold water from one of the "tanks" below them. Then, as he went up to take his rations, he sung out gaily to Ned:

"Here, Ned, my boy. We ought to have a sentry posted to present arms to the captain when he comes in. Get your rifle and mount guard until I get through here." And Ned, proud to be so employed, and out in the Indian country, too, was presently pacing up and down on the side nearest the road, with all the gravity and importance of a veteran soldier.

Pike made great pretence of having a tremendous appetite and made little Nell help him to coffee twice, refusing to take sugar except from her hand. Once during his repast, poor old Kate came forth from behind the ambulance, and with her apron to her eyes slowly approached them, but the trooper sternly warned her back, saying no word but pointing significantly to the ambulance. He did not mean to have the little ones upset by the nurse's lamentations. His "square meal" finished, he asked Nellie to see to the breakfast for her father being carefully kept in readiness and then, sauntering off towards the road, called Jim to follow him.

Then, while they were apparently examining the bolts of the baggage wagon, he gave the darkey his instructions.

"Jim, I don't know when the captain will get back or how far he's gone, but I haven't a dread or fear of any kind now. Up there where you see that big gray rock I've found a cave that is the most perfect defensive position I ever saw. No bullet can reach it from any point, and on the contrary, from the mouth of the cave, we command the whole hillside. Now if those Apaches are bound to follow, they ought to be along here about noon. If the captain gets here in plenty of time we'll pull out for the Chiquito. If he doesn't I mean to move the whole outfit up to the cave. I want you now to roll and strap all the blankets; to get the provisions and everything of that kind in shape so that we can easily 'pack' them, then I'm going back to the top of the rock to keep a look out. I can see way beyond Jarvis Pass, and if the Indians are following I'll spot them before they get within ten miles of us. See?"

Quarter of an hour later Pike was once more on the top of the rock. First he glanced at his watch. Just nine o'clock. Then he sprawled at full length upon the blanket he had brought with him, levelled his glasses and, resting his elbows on the rock, gazed long and earnestly over the winding road. Presently he sat up, whipped off the red silk handkerchief about his neck, carefully wiped the eye and object glasses of his binocular and his own tired old eyes and, once more prone on his stomach, gazed again; then twisted the screw a trifle as though to get a better focus; gazed still another time; lowered the glass; rose to his knees, his eyes gleaming brilliantly and his teeth setting hard; once more levelled the glass and looked with all his soul in his eyes and then slowly let the faithful binocular fall to the blanket by his side as he spoke aloud:

"By Jove! They're coming."

CHAPTER V

THE PRISONER

What Pike saw, far over on the plateau towards Jarvis Pass would perhaps have attracted no attention from tourist or casual looker through a field glass, but to him—an old trooper, Indian fighter and mountaineer, it conveyed a world of meaning. Against the dark background of that distant ridge and upon the dun-colored flat along which the road meandered, the old corporal could just make out a number of dingy white objects—mere specks—bobbing and twinkling in the blazing sunshine. Nothing of the kind had been there when he looked before and he knew only too well what it meant. Those dirty white specks were the breech-clouts and turbans worn by nearly all the Tonto warriors in preference to any other head-gear or clothing, —a cheap cotton cloth being always kept in abundant supply at the agencies solely for their use. Some of them, it is true, wore no turban at all, their luxuriant growth of coarse black hair tumbling about their shoulders and trimmed off in a "bang" just level with their fierce, beady eyes, being all the head covering they needed. But the breech-clout was universal and some few even wore loose cotton shirts. These, with the moccasin and leggin invariably worn, the leggin generally in a dozen folds at the ankle, made the war toilet of the intractable Tonto. There was none of the finery of the proud warriors of the plains— the Sioux, Cheyenne or Crow—but for all that, when those

Charles King

Apaches took to the war-path, the soldiers used to say, "It meant business."

"They will be here in three hours at the rate they're coming; three short hours, too, for those beggars can keep up a jog trot all day long. Now for it! captain or no captain."

With that brief soliloquy Pike slid down from his perch, and for the second time that morning made his way down the hillside and back to camp. Here he found Kate and the children as full of eager and anxious inquiry about papa as before, and could only comfort them by saying that the mules must have run far to the south and were proving more than ordinarily obstinate about coming back. Still, he said, papa is sure to be here before noon, and indeed he hoped, and more than half believed, that such would be the case. Knowing the danger that menaced his little ones, it could not be that the captain would not use every endeavor to get back to them before the Indians could reach the Pass.

Jim had obeyed his instructions to the letter. There were the two big rolls of blankets, securely strapped; there were the supplies; the bacon, bread, *frijoles*, coffee, sugar, canned meats and vegetables. Even some jams and jellies for the children, together with the coffee pot, skillets, plates, cups and saucers all stowed away in the big iron kettle that hung under the wagon and in a pail or two, ready to be plumped into the ambulance if a start was to be made for the river, or "toted" up the hill if the order was to take to the cave. And then the irrepressible propensity of the negro had cropped out again. There lay Black Jim peacefully snoring in the sunshine, oblivious of all danger.

"Now, Kate, as the captain has my horse, I'm going to borrow his awhile," said Pike. "I want to ride down the range a little way and see if I can't help him home with the mules. You are perfectly safe here. Just as safe, at least, as you would be if I were with you. I wouldn't go and leave you if it were not absolutely necessary, as I believe it to be. You'll take care of her, won't you, Ned, my boy?"

The little fellow looked up bravely. "Nellie and I aren't afraid," he said. "Only we do want papa to come and get something to eat. Jim told me not to let the fire go out and I put on a little dry wood now and then."

But Kate sat with her apron to her eyes, rocking to and fro in speechless misery and dread, Nellie striving vainly to comfort her. All unconscious of the coming peril, the little ones were fearless and almost content. They had no sympathy for their old nurse's terror. Pike stopped and spoke once again to Kate before riding away, but in ten minutes, mounted on a fresh and spirited horse, with his rifle athwart the pommel and the field glasses in their case swinging by their strap from his shoulder, he cantered boldly up the Pass and was soon well out upon the open plain. His idea was to ride straight out to the west along the road, five or six miles and more if necessary, scour the country southward with the glasses in search of Captain Gwynne, and if he saw nothing of him to get near enough to the advancing Apaches to see about how large a party they were, then to whirl about, put spurs to his horse, ride like the wind for camp, get Kate, the children, Jim and the blankets and provisions up to the cave and be all ready for the Tontos when they came. "Gregg" was curveting and prancing even now, eager for a gallop, but Pike's practised hand kept him down to a moderate gait and in this way he rode steadily westward towards a distant rise in the midst of the undulating plateau, and there he felt confident he could see all that there was to be seen. It was just ten o'clock when he reined in at the top of a gentle ascent and unslung his glasses. First he looked towards Jarvis Pass to see how far away were the enemy and how many in number. Despite the windings of the road and occasional stunted trees or bushes, the first glance through the binocular placed them at once. Yes, there they were in plain view—certainly not more

Charles King

than four miles away. Not only could he count the breech-clouts and turbans now, but the swarthy, sinewy bodies could be made out as they came bobbing at their jog trot along the trail. "Twenty-five in that party at least," muttered Pike, "and coming for all they're worth. But what on earth are they bunched so for? There seems to be half a dozen in a clump, right in the middle of the road." Long and earnestly he studied them; a strange, worried expression coming into his face. Then, just as he had done at the rock, Pike wiped the glasses and his own eyes, and then gazed again.

"By heaven!" he muttered at last. "That's a prisoner, sure as fate, that they are lashing and goading along ahead of them. Who on earth can it be? Oh, God grant it isn't the captain!" Rapidly then he swept the plateau southward, searching the foothills of the range south of the Pass, his whole heart praying for some glimpse of horse and rider, but it was all unavailing. Then, with one more look at the coming foe, poor Pike turned, with almost a groan of misery and anxiety, gave "Gregg" one touch of the spur and a flip of the reins, and away he flew at full speed back to his duty at the Pass. One minute he reined in as he neared the gorge to note the direction taken by Manuelito. There were the tracks of the two mules, and running southward out across the open plain, but the captain had turned south almost the instant he had got out from among the foothills. His trail started parallel with the range. Surely then he ought to have returned to camp by this time.

And now, as once again he neared the little fastness in the rocks, Pike drew rein and rode at easy, jaunty lope down the Pass. He would not alarm his charges by hoof-beat that indicated the faintest haste. When he and "Gregg" came into view no one of the anxious watchers could have dreamed for an instant that he had seen a horde of fierce Apaches hastening to overtake them.

"Just as I thought," he sung out cheerily. "The captain went right down the range to the south and the mules strayed off across the plateau, so they missed each other and he won't come back till he gets them. It's all right, but I expect he's pretty hungry by this time." Then, springing from the saddle, he picked little Nell up in his arms:

"And now, baby, you want to see the beautiful house I found for you, don't you? We'll all go up and take a look at it and have lunch up there—and lots of fun—while we wait for papa." And then with a kiss he set her down and stalked over to where Jim was still snoring in the sunshine!

"Wake up, Jim!" he cried, giving him a lively shake or two. "Wake up and give me a lift here. Nellie wants to see her stone house."

It took some hard shaking—it generally does—to rouse the darkey from his slumber, but Jim presently sat up, rubbed his eyes, looked around him, and then, as though suddenly recovering his faculties, sprang to his feet.

"Unsaddle 'Gregg' and put the saddle, bridle and blanket with the other stuff, Jim," whispered Pike. "We must take our horse equipments and harness with us. We've got to move up to the cave. No hurry, mind you. You fetch the blankets first. I'll carry Nellie."

Then calling to Ned to bring his Ballard—there were lots of squirrels up the hill—a fiction that can hardly have been very heavily charged against him, Pike quickly lifted Nellie to his shoulders and strode off up the rocks. "You come, too, Kate. It's quite a climb but it'll do you good," he shouted, and presently he had his whole procession strung out behind him and clambering from bowlder to bowlder. Long before they reached the ledge they had to let poor Kate recover breath and, after one or two halts of this kind, Pike sent Jim ahead with the blankets and bade him come back at once and tow, push or "boost" the stout Irishwoman to their destination. At last the rock was reached, Ned and Nellie shouting with delight over the wonderful cave and speedily making themselves at home in its inmost recesses, Kate breathless and exhausted and bemoaning the fates that brought her on such an uncanny trip. The blankets were spread out on the smooth surface of the rock within the great, gloomy hollow. Jim was sent down for another load while Pike clambered up to his watch-tower and took a long look with his glass. The Indians had not yet reached the rise from which he had counted their numbers at ten o'clock.

In an hour more all the provisions they could need for several days, more blankets and pillows, all the arms and ammunition, all the harness and horse equipments had been lugged up to and safely stowed in and about the cave. "They'll burn the wagons, blast them!" muttered Pike to himself, "but we can leave the horses there. They won't harm them because they will want them to get away with in case they find the cavalry on their trail. The chances are the horses can be recovered, but darn me if I'll let 'em have saddle, bridle or harness to run off anything with." Then once more he had climbed to his post and was diligently watching the road, while Jim, obedient to orders, was rolling rocks and bowlders around to the opening of the cave.

"What's thim for?" demanded Kate.

"Corporal Pike's goin' to build a wall here to keep out the bears," said Jim, with lowered voice and a significant glance at the children prattling happily together at the back of the cave, and poor Kate knew 'twas no use asking questions.

And now, through the glasses, Pike could see the Tontos gathered on the low hillock which had been the western limit of his morning ride. They seemed to have come suddenly upon "Gregg's" hoof prints and to have halted for consultation. Full half an hour they tarried there and the children began to clamor for the promised luncheon. Sauntering down by a roundabout way the veteran picked up an armful of dry twigs, sticks and dead boughs and tossed them down at the mouth of the cave. Then, behind the rock, he built a small fire of the dryest twigs he could find, explaining that he didn't want smoke in the dining room, and soon had his skillet heating and his kettle of water at the boil. Jim was directed to cook all that was needed for luncheon and to have plenty for the captain, who would be sure to come back mighty hungry in course of the afternoon, and the corporal was speedily at his post again. What could it mean? The Tontos were still hanging about that little hill six miles out there on the plain. Was it possible they had abandoned the pursuit?

Noon came; one o'clock, two o'clock. They had all had luncheon, and Pike had been scrambling up and down the rock like a monkey, and still there was no forward movement of the foe. Every time he looked they were still lounging or squatting, so he judged, about the stunted trees on the knoll, and there was nothing to explain the delay. It must have three o'clock when at last the binocular told him they were again in motion and coming rapidly toward him. He could see the dirty white breech-clouts floating in the breeze and could almost distinguish the forms of the warriors themselves. Leaving his glass on the top of the ledge he slid down to the base again, called quietly to Jim, and the two men set to work to build their breastwork. Bowlders big and little, rocks of every possible shape and size were all around them, and in three-quarters of an hour they had a stout parapet fully four feet high, whose loopholes commanded the approach up the hillside, and yet were secure from fire from above, below or either flank. Then back he went to his watch-tower.

The instant he adjusted the glass and levelled it at the road, Pike gave vent to an expletive that need not be recorded here, but that indicated in him a most unusual degree of excitement. No wonder. The Tontos were now in plain view—only two miles and a half out there on the plain, —and though they were spread out, as a rule, to the right and left of the road, quite a number of them came jogging along the road itself, and right in the midst of these, led by an Indian in front and guarded by two or three in rear— were the missing mules. Even at that distance Pike could swear to them. On they came, rapidly, relentlessly, well knowing that even if their human prey had escaped them the big wagon must be somewhere about the Pass and loaded still with provisions. Nearer—nearer jogged the leaders; but now the old trooper was carefully studying a dark object on the back of the foremost mule—a pack of some kind—and marvelling what it could be,—wondering, too, what they had done with their prisoner. He was sure they had one as they came along that morning. At last they were within a mile of the heights and the western entrance to the Pass, and now their speed slackened. They began opening out farther and farther to the right and left, and the nearer they came to the foothills the slower and steadier became their advance. The mules and their attendants were kept well in the background and for the life of him Pike could not tell what that queer looking "pack" could be. Slowly, steadily, the Tonto skirmish line came on. Every moment brought them nearer to the mouth of the Pass. The sun was low down in the west and threw long shadows of the approaching foe before them. Little by little, crouching, almost crawling, the more daring spirits among them would give a spring and a rapid run to the front of forty or fifty yards. Evidently they expected to be greeted with a sharp fire somewhere about the Pass, and did not dare push ahead in their usual order. And now they had reached the entrance to the defile. Two or three, as flankers, remained well out to the right and left among the trees; two or three stole cautiously ahead down the road. Pike watched their every move, yet found himself every few seconds fixing his gaze on that foremost mule now placidly cropping the scant herbage while the skirmish line pushed ahead. Presently a signal of some kind was given and repeated. The Indians in charge of the mules hastened with them to the mouth of the Pass, and as they did so, that singular pack came closer under Pike's powerful glass.

"It's their prisoner," he uttered. "They have driven and goaded him until he fainted from exhaustion. Then they had to wait for the mules to be brought up to the hillock— then lashed the poor fellow upon the back of one of them and pushed ahead." For some purpose of their own they were keeping him alive, and death by fearful torture was something to be looked forward to in the near future. The corporal continued to gaze as though fascinated until the leading mule got almost under him, and then he gave a groan of helplessness and misery as he exclaimed, "My God! My God! It's Manuelito!"

CHAPTER VI

MANUELITO'S FATE

For ten minutes Pike remained at his post of observation on top of the rock, watching the Indians as they slowly and cautiously moved down the Pass in the direction of the abandoned camp. The children, worn out with their play, and the fatigues of the climb, were sleeping soundly in the little cave on the peak,—Nellie, with her fair head pillowed in patient Kate's lap. Black Jim, too, was lying where the sun shone full upon him, and snoring away as placidly as earlier in the morning.

Kate, far back in the cave, had no idea what was going on in the Pass below; but her soul was still filled with dread and anxiety. The old trooper knew well that just as soon as the Indians came to the wagons and found them abandoned, their first care would be to secure all the plunder from them possible. Then they would probably dispose of Manuelito after their own cruel designs; and then, if darkness did not come on in the meantime, they would probably begin their search for the fugitives. There would be no difficulty to Indian trailers in following their track up the mountain side; of this Pike was well assured. But the wary old trooper had taken the precaution, every time that he and Jim had gone to and from the camp, to take a roundabout path, so as to bring their trail around the base of the mountain in front of the cave, and in this way the Indians in following would come directly in front of their barricade at the mouth and from sixty to a hundred yards down the hill and within easy range and almost sure shot of the defenders.

And now, peering down into the road far below, Pike could see that the leading Indians had come in sight of the big baggage wagon and that they were signalling to those in the rear, for almost instantly three or four sinewy, athletic young fellows sprang up among the trees and bowlders on the north side of the Pass, and crouching like panthers, half crawling, half springing, they went flitting from rock to rock or tree to tree until lost to the view of the lone watcher on the great ledge, but it was evident that their purpose was to reconnoitre the position from that side, as well as to surround the objects of their pursuit should they still be there. Almost at the same instant, too, an equal number of the Tontos came leaping like goats a short distance up the slope towards Pike's unconscious garrison, but speedily turned eastward, and, adopting precisely the same tactics as those of their comrades across the road, rapidly, but with the utmost stealth and noiselessness, bore down on the abandoned nook.

"Mighty lucky we got out of that and found this," muttered Pike. "It won't be five minutes before they satisfy themselves that there is no one left to defend those wagons or the horses—and the moment they realize it there'll be a yell of delight."

Sure enough! After a brief interval of silence, there came from below a shout of exultation, answered instantly by triumphant yells from the Indians in the roadway, and echoed by a wail of mortal terror from poor Kate, crouching below in the cave. Pike lost no time in sliding down the rocks and striving to comfort her. Nellie, clinging to her nurse, was terrified by the sounds. Little Ned, pale, but with his boyish face set and determined, grasped once more his little Ballard rifle, and looked up in the corporal's face as much as to say: Count on me for one of your fighting men! Trembling, shivering and calling on the blessed saints, poor Kate stood there wringing her hands, the very person-ification of abject fright. Jim, coming around to the mouth of the cave, spoke sternly to her; told her she ought to be ashamed of herself for setting so bad an example to little Nell. "Look at Ned," he said, "see how the little man behaves; his father would be proud of him." And then Pike spoke up. "Don't worry, don't be so afraid, Kate; they have got all they want just now. They'll just plunder and gorge themselves with food, and then they will have Manuelito to amuse themselves with. It is getting too late in the day for them to attempt to follow us. They have got too much to occupy themselves with anyhow. Don't you worry, old girl; if they do come this way, as they may to-morrow morning, we'll give them a dose that will make them wish they had never seen a Yankee."

The Indian shouts redoubled; every accent was that of triumph. They were evidently rejoicing over the rich find in the ambulance and the baggage wagon. Of course a great deal of property had been left there for which Pike's party would have no possible use up here in the cave, and this included plenty of food. The horses, too, delighted the Tontos, and, as Pike said, they would doubtless be occupied some little time with the division of the spoils, and longer in having a grand feast.

Looking down the road he could see the two mules browsing peacefully side by side, Manuelito still lashed to the back of one of them. Two young Indians stood guard over him and their four-footed captives; but even these fellows were by no means forgotten, for every now and then Pike could see their friends running back to them with something to eat and, after exchanging a word or two, hurrying again to the wagons.

After a while poor Kate, partially assured by Pike's words,

but more shamed into silence by the bravery of little Ned, subsided into a corner of the cave, and there seated herself, moaning and weeping, but no longer making any outcry. Pike decided that it would be necessary for him to go once more to his watch-tower, and as far as he could, watch the programme of the Apaches the rest of the day. Before starting, however, he called up Jim and gave him his instructions: "You see that the sun is almost down. The chances are that they will be so much interested in what they have found that darkness will settle down upon us before they fairly get through with their jubilee. Then, again, it may be that the bloody hounds will have some fun of their own with poor Manuelito to-night. I've no sympathy for the scoundrel, but I can't bear the idea of one who has served with us so long being tortured before our very eyes. We can't help it, however, there are only two of us here, and our first object is to protect these poor little children, and that wretched old Kate of a nurse there. Stay here with your rifle behind the barricade. I'll whistle if any Indian attempts to follow our trail; then I'll come down here as quickly as possible. But keep a bright lookout yourself. Watch those trees down there to the front. Note everything occurring along the road as far as you can see. There goes one of the beggars back to that point now. Even in the midst of their fun they don't neglect precautions. See! he's going to climb up there on that little hill just where I was watching this morning. Yes, there he goes. Now you will see him lie down flat when he gets to the top, and peer over the rocks to the west. What he is looking out for, I don't know, but it may be that they expect the cavalry even more than we do. They possibly have had signal fires from the reservation warning them that the cavalry have already left the Verde. I hope and pray they have. Now, keep up your grit, Jim; don't let anything phaze you. If you want help, or see anything, whistle, and I'll come down."

Already it was growing darker down the gorge. Pike could see that the Apaches had lighted a fire in the road close to the wagons. Evidently they were going to begin some cooking on their own account, and were even now distributing the provisions they had found. Two of them had released Manuelito from the mule, and the poor devil was now seated, bound and helpless, on a rock by the roadside, looking too faint and terrified to live. The captain's field glass revealed a sorry sight to the old soldier's eyes as he peered down at the little throng of savages about the baggage wagon, now completely gutted of its contents; and though he despised the Mexican as a traitor and thief and coward, it was impossible not to feel compassion for him in his present awful plight. There was something most pitiable in the fellow's clasped hands and abject despair. He had lived too long in Arizona not to know the fate reserved for prisoners taken by the Indians, and he knew, and Pike knew, that, their hunger once satisfied, the chances were ten to one they would then turn their attention entirely to their captive, and have a wild and furious revel as they slowly tortured him to death.

The sun had gone down behind the range, far over to the west, as Pike reached once more the top of his watch-tower, and every moment the darkness deepened down the Pass. Up here he could not only see the baggage wagon in the road, but the top of the ambulance, and two of the horses were also visible, and occasionally the lithe forms of the Tontos scurrying about in the firelight. Evidently the old cook fire in the cleft of the rocks had been stirred up and was now being utilized by half the band, while the others toasted the bacon and roasted *frijoles* down in the road. The yells had long since ceased. Many of the warriors were squatting about the baggage wagon gnawing at hard bread or other unaccustomed luxuries, but those at the ambulance were chattering like so many monkeys and keeping up a hammering, the object of which Pike could not at first imagine, until he suddenly remembered the locked box under the driver's seat, the key of which was always carried by the captain. Then a flash of hope shot over him as he recalled the fact that when they left their station Captain Gwynne had stowed away in there three or four bottles of whiskey or brandy. It would take them but a little while, he knew, to break into the enclosure, and then there would be a bacchanalian scene.

"Oh, that it were a barrel instead of a bottle or two," groaned Pike. "As it is there's just enough to exhilarate the gang and keep them, singing and dancing all night; but a barrel!—that would stupefy them one after another and Jim and I could have gone down and murdered the whole crowd. Not one of 'em would ever have known what hurt him."

Ha! a sound of crashing, splitting wood. A rush, a scuffle—then a yell of triumph and delight. Every Indian in the roadway sprang to his feet and darted off up the rocks to swell the chorus at the ambulance. Even Manuelito's guard left his prisoner to take care of himself and ran like a deer to claim his share of the madly craved "fire water." A few years before and most of them hardly knew its taste, but some of their number had more than once made "John Barleycorn's" acquaintance and had told wondrous tales of its effects. In less than a minute, with the single exception of their sentry on the hill, every Tonto was struggling, shouting, laughing and leaping about the family wagon, and Pike knew from the sounds that the captain's little store of liquor was rapidly disappearing. Every moment the noise waxed louder and fiercer as the deep potations of the principal Indians did their poisonous work. There were shrill altercations, vehement invective and reproach; Pike even hoped for a minute that there had been enough after all to start them fighting among themselves, but the hope was delusive. All was gloom and darkness now in the Pass except immediately around the two fires. He could no longer see Manuelito or the mules, but suddenly he heard a sound of a simultaneous rush and an instant after with hideous shouts and yells the whole band leaped into view and went tearing down into the road and up to the rocks where their helpless prisoner still sat bound and helpless—more dead than alive—and Pike heard the shriek of despair with which the poor fellow greeted his now half crazy captors.

"My God!" groaned the old soldier, "it is awful to have to lurk here and make no move to help him. He would have cut all our throats without a twinge of conscience, but I can't see him tortured nor can I lift a hand to save him. And here's Kate, and those poor little ones. They can't help hearing his cries and shrieks. What an awful night 'twill be for them! No use of my staying up here now. I must go down to them."

Far back in the black recesses of the cave he found them, —Nellie trembling and sobbing with her head pillowed in Kate's lap and covered with a shawl so as to shut out, if possible, the awful sounds from below. The Irishwoman, too, was striving to stop her ears and was at the same time frantically praying to all the saints in the calendar for help in their woeful peril, and for mercy for that poor wretch whose mad cries and imprecations rang out on the still night air even louder than the yells of his captors. Manful little Ned sat close by his sister's side, patting her arm from time to time with one hand while he clung to his rifle with the other. The boy did not shed a tear, though his voice trembled and his lips quivered as he answered Pike's cheery words. Jim knelt at his post at the stone breastwork keeping vigilant watch, though his teeth chattered despite his best efforts, and his eyes were doubtless bulging out of their sockets.

"You mustn't be sitting here all in the dark," said Pike. "Keep up a little fire, Ned, my boy. It's so far back and so far up the hill that the Indians cannot possibly see the light it may make even were they to come around to the east side of the mountain. They won't to-night, though. They've found papa's stock of whiskey and brandy and are already half drunk. They'll lie around there all night long and never come hunting for us until after sunrise to-morrow, if they do then. We'll just have fun with these fellows until the cavalry come from Verde, as come they will, I haven't a doubt, now that papa has found that he was cut off and has ridden back on the trail to meet and hurry the troops. He knows well that you and Jim and I could take care of Nellie and stand off these beggars until he could reach us. Now, light the lantern and stow it in that niche yonder. And you, Kate, lie down and cover yourself and the children with blankets. I'm going out where I can watch what they're doing."

So saying, Pike took his rifle and the field glasses and, after a word with Jim, passed around to the east front of the ledge. It was too dark to enable him to venture down the bowlders, or to attempt to climb again to the top of the rock, but he found a spot among the stunted trees from which he could just see the back part of the baggage wagon and the Apaches flitting about it in the light of their fire. Leveling his glasses he could make out that several of the Indians were grouped about some object in the road, and presently one or two came running to the spot with buckets of water which they dashed over a prostrate form. It was Manuelito, who had probably fainted dead away.

Then, as the Mexican apparently began to recover his senses, he was lifted roughly from the ground and borne, moaning and feebly struggling, towards the wagon. Into this he was tossed head foremost, so that only his feet and legs were visible to the anxious watcher up the hill. Securely bound, and already half dead from the tortures inflicted on him, unable to move hand or foot, the poor wretch lay there, alternately praying and weeping. What the next move of the Apaches would be was not long a matter of doubt. The whole band, with the exception of their sentinels, were now dancing and leaping about their captive, singing some devil-inspired chant, which occasionally gave place to yells of triumph. Presently the younger men began piling up wood under the back of the wagon—under the Mexican's manacled feet; and then brands and embers were thrust underneath. Pike turned sick with horror and helplessness at the sight, for he knew instantly what it meant. The wagon was to be the wretched Manuelito's funeral pyre. They meant to burn him to death by inches. Suddenly a bright flame leaped up from the bottom of the stack of fuel; broader, brighter, fiercer it grew until it lapped up over the floor of the wagon. A scream of agony rang through the Pass, answered by jeering laughter and fiendish yells. The next minute the whole band were circling round the wagon in a wild war-dance; their yells, their savage song, completely drowned the shrieks of the tortured man. The whole wagon was soon a mass of flames, and more fuel was added. Presently the rear axle came down with a crash, sending showers of sparks whirling through the night air, and Pike turned away faint and trembling.

Another instant, however, and every faculty was on the alert, every nerve strung to its highest tension, and the old soldier sprang back to the cave in answer to Jim's call.

"Look!" whispered the negro. "Look down there! There's some one moving among those rocks."

CHAPTER VII

PIKE'S STRANGE DREAM

Kneeling behind their rocky barrier the two men silently peered into the darkness down the hill. The great ledge of rock under which they were hiding concealed from their view the burning fires of the Indians down in the roadway to the east. But the reflection of the fire could be plainly seen on the rocks and trees on the north side of the Pass. Here and there stray beams of light shot through the firs and cedars and stunted oaks that lay below them among the bowlders; and somewhere down among these little trees, watchful Jim declared that he had seen something white moving cautiously and stealthily to and fro. Pike closely questioned him, whispering his inquiries so as not to catch the ears of Kate or the children, but Jim stoutly declared that he could not be mistaken. He had marked it twice, moving from place to place, before he had quit his post and called to the corporal to come and verify for himself what he was sure he had seen. For a few moments Pike thought that it might be the Apache sentinel who had, possibly, left his position on the little hill across the road, and was seeking on his own account some clue to the whereabouts of the fugitives from the camp. Pike had seen one or two Indians running up the road to where the sentinel was stationed in order to give him some of the plunder which they had taken from the wagon, and it was now so dark that he could no longer see objects out on the plain, and, as he could hear approaching horsemen just as well on this side of the road as on that, it was quite possible that this Indian was the cause of Jim's warning.

Several minutes passed without either of them seeing anything. Then suddenly Jim's hand was placed on the corporal's arm, and in a low, tremulous voice he whispered: "Look! Look!"

Following with his eyes the direction indicated by Jim's hand, Pike could just see, probably two hundred or two hundred and fifty yards away down the hillside, something dirty white in color, very slowly and very stealthily creeping from one bowlder to another. The tops and crests of the trees and bowlders, as has been said, were tinged by the light of the fires still burning down in the roadway. The Indian yells were gradually ceasing as, one after another, seemingly overcome by the liquor that they had been drinking, they subsided into silence. A number of them, however, still kept up their monotonous dance, varied every now and then by a yell of triumph; but the uproar and racket was not to be compared with what had been going on during the torture to which Manuelito had been subjected before they had mercifully, though most horribly, put an end to his sufferings.

Nothing but the embers of the wagon and the unconsumed iron work, of course, now remained in the road. Pike judged too that the ambulance had been burned, and that nothing remained of that. But all thought as to what was going on among the Indians in the Pass was now of little account as compared with the immediate presence of this object below him. Could it be one of the Apaches? Could it be the sentinel from the other side? Its stealthy movements and the noiseless way in which it seemed to flit from rock to rock gave color to his supposition, and yet it appeared unnatural to Pike that any one of the Indians should separate himself from his comrades and go on a still hunt in the dead of the night for traces of their hated foes.

"I cannot see it now," whispered Jim. "Where is he gone?"

"Behind that big rock that you see touched by the firelight down yonder. Our trail is just about half way. Look! There it is again! Nearer, too, by fifty yards. I wish he'd get on top of one of those bowlders where the light would strike him. Then we might make him out. By Jove! He's coming up the hill. Whatever you do, don't fire. I'll tend to him."

With straining eyes they watched the strange, stealthy approach of the mysterious object. Every now and then it would totally disappear from sight and then, a moment or two afterwards, could again be dimly seen, crouching along beside some big rock or emerging behind the thick branches of some stunted tree. Nearer it came until Pike was sure it must have reached the "trail" they had made in their journeys up and down the hill.

"I never saw an Apache that could move about in the dark as quickly as that fellow. Jim, by Jimminy, I'll bet it's no Indian at all!"

"What is it, then?" muttered Jim, whose teeth would chatter a little. He had all a darkey's dread of "spooks" and was more afraid of a possible ghost than an actual Tonto.

"That's a lynx or a wild-cat, man! They have a dingy white coat to their backs, in places at least, and you've only stirred up some mighty small game. See here, Jim, you're getting nervous. I'll have to call Ned out here with his little Ballard to take your place if you are going to—There! What did I tell you?"

A heap of fresh fuel—probably dry cedar boughs—had just been thrown on the coals by some of the determined dancers down in the road and a broad glare of firelight illumined the Pass. Again the rocks and trees down in front of the cave were brilliantly tinged, and, as though determined to have a good look at these strange "goings on," there suddenly leaped from the darkness and appeared in view upon the flat top of one of the biggest bowlders a little four-footed creature gazing with glowing eyes upon the scene below.

"There's your Indian, James, my boy," softly laughed Pike and, turning, he called back into the cave:

"Ned, are you asleep?"

"No," was the prompt answer. "Do you want me, Pike?"

"Come here and I'll show you a pretty shot for your Ballard."

Ned was at his side in an instant, bringing his little rifle with him, and the old soldier pointed down the hill.

"That's what Jim took for an Apache," he said.

"So did you, Pike; you needn't try to make fun of me," was Jim's answer, half surly, half glad, because his fears were now removed.

"Is it a panther?" whispered Ned. "Oh!—can't I take a pop at him?"

"Not a shot. It would simply be telling those blackguards where we were hiding and spoil all the fun I expect to have in the morning. That's no panther; they have a tawny hide; but it's the biggest catamount or wild-cat I ever set eyes on. Now go back to Kate, bundle up in your blankets and keep warm and go to sleep. Jim and I stand guard to-night."

And, obediently, the boy crept away. Pike looked after him

with moistening eyes—all his jovial, half-laughing manner changing in an instant.

"God bless the little man! He's as brave and plucky as a boy could be, and hasn't so much as whimpered once," muttered the ex-corporal to himself. "What would I not give to know where his father was this night!"

Then he turned to Jim who had somewhat sulkily drawn away to the other end of the little parapet.

"Come back, Jim, my boy. I didn't mean to hurt your feelings," he said. "You were perfectly right in keeping such close watch on everything and anything the least suspicious and I was wrong if I ridiculed it. Now we've got to divide the night between us. You lie down at once and go to sleep. I'll keep guard till one or half past; then you relieve me until daybreak."

And Jim, nothing loth, crept back towards the glowing coals and rolled himself in his heavy blanket, leaving the old corporal to his solitary reflections, and these were of a character so gloomy, so full of anxiety and dread, that one only marvels how he was able to keep up, before Kate and the children, the appearance of jollity and confidence that had marked throughout this trying day his whole demeanor.

"I would give anything to know where the captain is to-night!" again he muttered as his weary eyes gazed over the jagged hillside below him. The Indian fires were waning again and the gleams of light on rock and tree were growing fainter and fainter. The sounds of savage revelry, too, were more subdued, though a hoarse, monotonous chant came up from below. As has been said, Pike's watch-tower and fortress was fully a quarter of a mile south of the road and about a third of a mile from the abandoned camp, but in the absolute silence that reigned in every other quarter the sounds from the Apache war-dance in that clear mountain air were almost distinctly audible. The awful groans and cries of Manuelito were still ringing in his ears, and, to himself, the old soldier confessed that his nerve was not a little tried by the fearful sights and sounds of the early evening. It was poor preparation for the fight that he felt morally certain would speedily follow the rising of the morrow's sun, but Pike had been through too many an Indian war and in too many tight places before to "lose his grip," as he expressed it, now.

"If I only had those poor little kids safe with their father nothing would suit me better than to be here with four or five of the old 'Troop' and let the whole of the Apache nation try to rout me out," he said to himself. "Even as it is, I'm blood-thirsty enough now, after what I've seen and heard to-night, to be impatient for their attack. By gad! we've got a surprise in store for them if only Jim don't get stampeded."

Turning to listen for sounds from his little garrison, Pike could distinguish two that were audible and that prevailed above all or any others: Kate was tearfully moaning and praying aloud; Jim placidly snoring.

"That nigger could lie down and go to sleep, by thunder, if he knew the world was coming to an end in less than an hour. I'll have to watch here till nearly dawn and have the strongest coffee I can brew all ready for him or he'll be going to sleep on his post and letting those hounds crawl right upon us. Coffee's a good idea! I'll have some myself."

So saying the veteran stole back into the cave, noiselessly filled the battered coffee-pot and set it on the coals, said a few reassuring words to Kate and begged her to remember him in her prayers, laughed at her doleful and despairing reply and returned to his post.

All quiet. Even the wild-cat had disappeared and there was

now no longer light by which he could have detected the creature. Pike almost wished he hadn't gone, for, as he grimly said, the fellow might have been good company and kept him from getting sleepy. Little by little the Indian chant was getting drowsy and the weird dancers, some of the younger braves, tired of the sport when there were neither admiring squaws or approving old chiefs to look on. The chiefs in this case, of course, had consumed the greater portion of the whiskey and were now sleeping off its soporific effects, and the youngsters could only remain where they were, keep watch and ward against surprise, and make no move in any direction until their elders should be themselves again, unless the sudden coming of enemies should compel them to rouse their leaders from their drunken slumbers and skip like so many goats for the highest parts of the mountain.

Looking at his watch as he sipped his tin of coffee Pike noticed that it was now eleven o'clock. "Oh, if I only knew that all was well with the captain," he muttered. "And if I only knew where Sieber and the cavalry were to-night."

Not until after two o'clock in the morning did the old soldier decide that it was time to "turn over the command" and seek a little rest himself. He knew that he would not be half fit for the responsibilities of the coming day unless he could get a few hours' sleep, and as Jim had now been snoring uninterruptedly for over four hours, Pike concluded to call him, give him some strong coffee and some sharp instructions, and put him "on post." It took no little shaking and kicking to rouse the boy, but presently he sat up, just as he had done at the ambulance, with the yawning inquiry, "What's the matter?"

"Nearly half-past two, Jim, and your turn for guard. Stir out here, now. Douse your head with some of this cold water. It will freshen you up. Then I'll give you a good tin of coffee."

Jim obeyed, and after stumbling stupidly around a moment, and then having a gourd or two of water dashed over his face and neck, he pronounced himself all right and proceeded to enjoy the coffee handed him.

"Now, Jim," said Pike, "the wild-cat's gone, and no Apaches will be apt to prowl up here to-night, but I want you to keep the sharpest lookout you ever did in all your life—not only over their movements down in the road, but for cavalry coming from the west. There's just no telling how soon those fellows may be out from Verde, and when they come we want to know it. The Indians have their sentries out, so they evidently expect them. Watch them like a hawk, but don't give any false alarm or make any noise. Let me sleep until it begins to get light, then call me. Now, can you do it?"

"Of course I can, corporal, but where are you going to sleep?"

"Right here by you. I'll hand your blankets and mine out by the parapet, so that if you want me, all you have to do is put out your hand. If you are chilly, or get so towards daybreak, throw that saddle blanket over your shoulders."

For a long time, despite fatigue and watching, Pike could not get to sleep. He lay there looking up at the stars shining in the clear heavens and thinking how peaceful, how far removed from strife or battle, they seemed to be. Then he kept an eye on Jim, and was glad to note that the darkey seemed alert and aware of his responsibilities, for every few minutes he would creep out and peer around the shoulder of the ledge where he could get a better view of anything going on down in the road, and, after half an hour of this sort of thing, he reported to Pike that he "reckoned the whole gang had gone to sleep down there." The old trooper assured him, however, that some must be on the alert and warned him to relax in no way his vigilance, and then at last wearied Nature asserted her rights, and the soldier fell asleep.

Four o'clock came,—five o'clock,—and there had been no sound from below. Then, far in the east the skies began to hoist their colors in honor of the coming Day God, and rich crimson and purple soon blended with the richer gold, and all around the rocky fastness the pale, wan light of the infant morn stole over rock and tree, and still old Pike slept, but not the deep, restful slumber of three hours before. He was dreaming, and his dreams were troubled, for his limbs were twitching; he rolled over and moaned aloud; inarticulate sounds escaped from his lips; but still, as one laboring with nightmare, he could not wake—could not shake off the visions that oppressed him. In his sleep he saw, and saw beyond possibility of doubt, that the Apaches were hurriedly rousing their comrades; that they were quickly picking up their rifles and then nimbly speeding up the rocks; that even as they came towards him up the mountain side several of their number went crouching along towards the east and eagerly watching the roadway through the Pass, and, following their fierce eyes, he could see, winding up the gorge, coming at a trot, a troop of the longed-for cavalry— coming not from the west, as he had expected, but from the direction of the magnificent sunrise that flashed on their carbines and tinged the campaign hats with crimson. At their head rode two officers, and one, he knew at once, must be his old captain, but why that bandage about his head? Why the rude sling in which his arm was carried? Plainly visible though they were to him, the Apaches were completely hidden from the approaching troops. Two minutes' ride brought the leaders to the smouldering ruins of the baggage wagon, at sight of which, and the charred and unrecognizable body in their midst, his captain had groaned aloud, then forced his "broncho" up the rocky path to where they had made their camp, and then, when he saw the ruined ambulance and all the evidences of Apache triumph, he reeled in his saddle and would have fallen headlong had not two stout troopers held him while their young lieutenant thrust a flask of brandy between the ashen lips; and then in his wild vision Pike saw them ride on and on up the road right beneath them—only a quarter of a mile away—never heeding, never looking for him and his precious charges. He strove to shout: he screamed aloud, yet only a suffocated groan seemed to issue from his lips; he shouted to Jim to fire and so attract their attention, but there was no response; and then, in his agony, he started up, wide awake in an instant, and, hurling off his blankets, seized his rifle and sprang to his feet.

Broad daylight; sunbeams dancing through the trees; and there, doubled up at the back of the parapet, lay that scoundrel Jim—asleep on guard. One vehement kick and curse he gave him: then peered over the barrier down the rocky hillside. God of heaven! what a sight met his eyes! The Apaches were almost on them.

CHAPTER VIII

THE CAPTAIN'S RIDE

It is high time now that we should hear something of Captain Gwynne himself, and leave for the time our little garrison in the cave at Sunset Pass. Let us follow the movements of the father for whom the children were so anxiously and tearfully praying.

Galloping away on Pike's horse in close pursuit, as he supposed, of Manuelito and the mules, the captain had turned south the moment he cleared the rocky buttresses that formed the western gateway to the Pass. He had reasoned that the Mexican would not dare go back along the road on which they came, because in so doing he must infallibly run straight into the Apaches, who were following in pursuit. Knowing, as did Pike, that Manuelito was well acquainted with the short cut through the mountains down to the valley of the Verde, miles to the south of the winding and roundabout way on which they were compelled to come by road; knowing, too, that this trail was far to the south of where they had seen the Indians' signal fires,—Gwynne's whole idea seemed to be that Manuelito would take the shortest line to reach that rough but easily known trail. He did not hesitate, then, a moment in turning short to the south, and riding confidently along to the western foothills, expecting every moment to hear the bray of the mules or the sound of their hoof beats. He knew that the moment these creatures heard the hoof beats of his own horse, they would be almost sure to signal. Just what to do with Manuelito himself, he had not yet determined; but it was his purpose to force him back to camp at the point of the pistol, if necessary; then to bind him to the wagon; make him drive, at least until they reached Fort Wingate over in New Mexico beyond the Navajo Reservation, and turn him over there to the military authorities for such disposition as they might choose to make of him. Of course, he would have no further employ-ment in Arizona, for his character was blasted forever. Mile after mile, however, the captain rode without hearing one of the anticipated sounds, and the further he rode the lighter it grew. Far down, to the south, now, he could dimly see objects that looked like four-footed creatures, moving rapidly. Unluckily, he had with him only a light, short-ranged pair of glasses, and he could not distinctly make out what they were; but believing that they could be nothing but Manuelito and the mules, he put spurs to his weary horse, and pushed rapidly in pursuit— wondering, however, how it was that the Mexican, with the slow-moving mules, could have got so far to the front. Five miles further he rode and by that time the sun was up above the mountains of New Mexico, over to the east, and lighting up the whole plateau to his right. By this time, too, the objects, of which he had been in pursuit, had totally disappeared from his sight, and looking around him he could see nowhere sign of hoof or any trail that would indicate that the mules had come that way. However, as he might be anywhere from ten yards to ten miles from the exact line Manuelito traveled, this gave him no concern. He decided that he would push on until he came upon the cavalry trail up which he had ridden a year before on an expedition with their good guide Sieber to Chevelon Fork. By this time, too, he knew that he must be twelve miles from camp, and that in all probability the Indians had left their position west of Snow Lake, and were already coming in pursuit. He dreaded to think of the peril in which his children might be; but he had every confidence in Pike; he believed in Jim's pluck and fighting qualities, and he reasoned that it would be one or two o'clock before the Indians could possibly reach the Pass, and that he could easily get back long before that time. Riding, therefore, still further to the south, he pursued his search for an hour longer, and then came suddenly upon a sight that thrilled his heart with hope and joy. Right before him, coming across the southern edge of the plateau, and winding up the mountains to the left, was an unmistakable cavalry trail, not more than a day or two old. Evidently some troop was out from Verde and had taken the old short cut to Chevelon Fork, expecting by that route to make the quickest time to the Sunset crossing of the Colorado River. In all probability this was one of the troops coming out in search of and to succor him and his party. Reining his jaded horse to the left, the captain rapidly followed on the trail. He reasoned that the four-footed creatures that he took to be the mules were in all probability a portion of the pack-train of the troop that had so recently passed along, or it might be one or two troopers who had been making scouts to the right or to the left of the trail, and were now following the main body. All thought of pursuing Manuelito further was abandoned. His sole object was to overtake, as quickly as possible, the little command of cavalry that he knew to be in his path, and then to guide them by the shortest line back to Sunset Pass, and to the defence of the dear ones there awaiting him. If he had good luck, he might catch them before they had gone many miles. The trail he knew would speedily lead him over into the valley of Chevelon Fork, and following this they would emerge on the east side of the mountain. Perhaps it might be fortunate that he did not overtake them until they were east of the range; for the Apaches would certainly not expect the cavalry to come from the Colorado side of the mountain; but would be looking for them from the west, and the chances, therefore, would be all the more in favor of their dealing them a crushing blow, and punishing them as they deserved for their assault on defenseless women and children.

On, on he rode, urging his horse as rapidly as it was possible for him to go over the rocky, broken trail. Two hours' ride brought him no nearer, apparently, to the comrades he was pursuing. Three hours' ride brought him down into the valley of Chevelon Fork and half way through the range. It was not until one o'clock that he found himself at such a point that he could look forward and see part of the country toward the Colorado Chiquito; but not a vestige of the cavalry or pack-train was anywhere in sight, and his horse was now so weary that he could only answer with a groan the touch of the spur, and could not by any possibility accelerate his speed. Two o'clock came, and the anxious father found himself, he knew not how many miles away from Sunset Pass,—away from the children so anxiously praying for him, and awaiting his coming.

He was growing faint from long fasting, and the horse was so jaded that the captain dismounted and was fairly towing him along behind him with the bridle rein. In this way they had slowly and painfully climbed a steep and rocky ascent where the trail seemed to make a short cut across a deep bend of the stream, and reaching the summit they stopped to rest, panting hard with fatigue. Again the captain resorted to his little glasses and looked long and eagerly over the broad stretch of country to the east, but it was all in vain. No living creatures were in sight.

Directly in front, the trail wound downwards over an incline so steep that it looked as though horses and mules could never have made those hoof tracks, but that only goats could have gone that way. The poor old bay looked piteously at his master as though imploring him not to force him to undertake that steep descent, but Gwynne could show no mercy now. He had come too far to turn back. His only hope, if he could not find the scouting party, was to make his way along the east side of the range back to the little camp in Sunset Pass. He prayed God to watch over and protect his little ones, and then, with almost a sob rising to his throat, he tried to speak cheerfully to poor "Mac;" he patted the drooping head of his faithful old servitor and, calling to him to follow, he pressed forward, and half sliding, half stepping, he began the steep descent. The poor horse braced his fore feet and stiffened his knees and came skating over the loose slate after him. All went tolerably well until they were about two hundred feet from the rushing waters of the fork, foaming and swirling over the rocks below, and there, coming upon a sharp point around which they had to make their way, Gwynne had taken only three or four steps downward and was about to turn and speak encouragingly again to "Mac," when the horse's fore feet seemed to shoot from under him; he rallied, gathered himself, stumbled, and then, plunging heavily forward, crashed down upon his master, rolled completely over him, and then went sliding and pawing desperately to the edge of the rocky precipice, over which he shot, a huge, living bowlder and fell with a thud upon the jagged rocks below. For some minutes Gwynne lay where he had been hurled, stunned and senseless; then he slowly revived, found that his left arm was severely wrenched and bruised, and that the blood was streaming from a long gash in his forehead. Slowly and painfully he made his way to the foot of the steep, bathed his head in the cool waters and bound it up as well as he could with his big silk handkerchief. He was fainter, weaker now, than he had been before, but never for an instant could he forget the little ones at the Pass.

"Oh, God help me and bring me back to them in time," he prayed; and then, holding his maimed left arm in his right hand, and with one backward look up the canon at the now lifeless carcass of poor "Mac," he staggered wearily on, following the trail of the cavalry.

Late that evening, just as darkness was settling down over the valley of the Colorado Chiquito, the soldiers of a little detachment, chatting gleefully around their bivouac fires and sipping their fragrant coffee, were startled by the

Charles King

sudden sight of a man with ghastly, blood-stained features and dress, who reeled blindly into their midst and then fell forward upon his face, to all appearances dead.

Some of them, believing Indians to be upon them, sprang for their arms; others bent to the aid of the stricken man. They turned him over on his back, brought water and bathed the blood from his face, and then a sergeant cried:

"My God! What can have happened? It's Captain Gwynne! Here, Murphy, call the lieutenant, quick!"

In an instant the young officer commanding the party came running to the scene and bent breathlessly over the senseless form.

"It is Captain Gwynne," he said; "bring more water. Go to my pack, one of you, and get the sponge you'll find there. Fetch me my flask, too. Which way did he come? Did none of you see?"

"None, sir. The first we knew he was right over us. He never spoke a word, but fell like a log."

And then the rough-looking, bearded, anxious faces hovered about the prostrate man. His heart-beats were so faint that the young officer was terribly alarmed. No surgeon was with the little party and he hardly knew what to do. The whiskey forced down Gwynne's throat seemed powerless to revive him. Full an hour he lay almost motionless, then little by little the pulse grew firmer and respiration audible. At last there was a long, deep sigh, but still he did not open his eyes. Consciousness returned only very slowly, and when Mr. Hunter had called him by name time and again and begged him to speak, he sighed even more deeply than before, the lids slowly drew back, and the almost sightless eyes looked feebly around. Then, with sudden flash of memory, the poor captain strove to rise. "My babies!" he moaned; "my babies!"

"Where did you leave them, captain? Tell us. I'll send for them instantly," said Hunter. "Sergeant, saddle up right off. This means something."

More whiskey, a long draught, and more cold water, presently revived him so that he could speak collectedly.

"I left them with Pike—in the Pass. My Mexican ran away with the mules—followed and found your trail—my horse fell on me and then rolled over a precipice—killed. I've come on foot ever since."

"Thank God, you're here safe anyhow! Now lie still. I'll leave a guard with you and we'll go as fast as we can through the darkness and find Ned and Nellie."

"No! no! I must go. I will go, too. See, I can stand. Give me a horse."

And so, finding him determined and rapidly regaining strength, Hunter made the captain eat all he could bear to swallow then, and, stowing more food in their saddle bags, away went the gallant little troop hurrying through the starlit night for Sunset Pass and rescue.

But the way was long; road or trail there was none. Over rugged height, through deep ravine, they forced their way, but not until all the sky was blushing in the east did they come to the old Wingate road, and the gloomy entrance to the Pass. Up they rode at a steady trot, Gwynne and Hunter leading, and, at a sudden turn of the road, far in towards the western side, their horses recoiled, snorting with fear, from a heap of smouldering embers, in the midst of which lay a fearful something,—the charred and hissing body of a human being. Gwynne groaned aloud at the sight and then drove his horse up a rocky pathway to the left, the others

Charles King

following. There lay the smoking ruins of an ambulance with scraps of clothing heaped about on every side, and here the stricken father's waning strength left him entirely. With one heartbroken cry, "My babies—my little ones. They are gone! gone!" he was only saved from falling by the prompt action of two stalwart troopers.

In ten minutes, supporting the fainting soldier as best they could, the detachment was marching rapidly westward.

"Sieber with the scouts can't be farther away than Jarvis Pass. We'll meet him," said Hunter to his sergeant, "and trail these Scoundrels to their holes."

His words were true. Before ten o'clock they had met, not only Sieber, but Turner's troop from Verde, coming full tilt, and Gwynne was now turned over to the doctor's care.

CHAPTER IX

THE ATTACK

Startled suddenly from his sleep, it was indeed a dreadful sight, and one calculated to shake the nerves of many an old soldier, that greeted Pike's eyes as he peered over the rocky parapet in front of him. One glance was sufficient. Looking down behind the wall, he seized Jim by the throat, shaking him vigorously and at the same time placing his other hand over his mouth so that he might make no outcry. "Wake up, Jim! Wake up! and see what your faithlessness has brought upon us! Look down the hill here! Look through that loophole and see what you've done!"

Terrified, with his eyes starting from their sockets, Jim obeyed, and his black face showed in an instant the full realization of the scene before him.

"Now, is your rifle all ready?" whispered Pike. "Don't rouse those poor little people in there until we have to. They must stay way back in the cave. Now, observe strictly what I tell you: I want you to aim at the taller of those two Indians who are the leaders. Do not fire until I give the word; but be sure you hit. Recollect now, you've got to fire down hill, and the bullets fly high. Aim below his waistband, then you'll probably strike him either through the heart or the upper chest. Now, go to your loophole and stay there. Are you ready, Jim?"

"I'm ready, boss. Just wait one minute until I get my rifle through here."

Kneeling beside his own loophole, Pike once more looked down the hill. Not over a hundred yards away—crouching along, following step by step the trail that he and Jim had made—pointing with their long bony fingers at every mark on the ground or upon the trees—two lean, keen-eyed, sinewy Apaches were slowly and silently moving up the mountain side in a direction that would take them diagonally across the front of the hill. Behind them, among the trees and bowlders, and spread out to the right and left, came others,—all wary, watchful, silent,—as noiseless and as stealthy in their movements as any panther could possibly be. Pike could see that they were armed mostly with rifles. He knew that very few of them had breech-loaders at that time; but still that there were some among them which they had obtained by murdering and robbing helpless settlers, or mail messengers.

With abundant ammunition close at hand, with the advantage of position and the fact that he meant to have the first fire, Pike calculated that the moral effect would be such that he could drive them back, and that they would not resume the attack until after a consultation among themselves. The two who were so far in front of the others were steadily approaching the little barricade, only the top of which could readily be seen from below and was hardly distinguishable from the general mass of rocks and bowlders by which it was surrounded.

He knew it could not be long, however, before the quick eyes of the Apaches detected it, and that they would know at once what it meant. "However," thought Pike, "before they see it those two villains in front will be near enough for us to have a sure shot, and then, I don't care how soon they know we're here. Now, Jim," he whispered, "watch your man!—recollect—you aim at that tall fellow on your own side,—I'll take the little, skinny cuss—the one who is just turning towards us now. They are not more than seventy-five yards away. Aim low!"—There was a moment of breathless silence. "Are you ready, Jim?" whispered Pike.

"Yes, all ready, corporal."

"All right!—One minute now—get you a good aim!—Draw your bead on him!—Wedge your rifle in the rock, if necessary! Got it?"

"I think so, corporal."

"All right then! *Fire!*"

Bang! bang! rang out almost simultaneously the reports of two rifles. The smoke floated upward. Pike and Jim had the good sense not to attempt to lift their heads or peer over the barriers, but to content themselves with looking through the loopholes. One look revealed the scene. "The little, skinny cuss," as Pike had called him, clasping his hands to his breast, had fallen head foremost among the rocks up which he was climbing. But the tall Indian, giving a spring like that of a cat, had leaped behind a bowlder full ten feet away from him, and the next instant,—bang! went his rifle, and a bullet whizzed overhead and struck, flattening itself upon the rocks.

"Oh, you've missed him, Jim," said Pike, reproachfully. "Now, look out for the others!"

The rest of the Apaches, hearing the shots, with the quickness of thought, had sprung for shelter behind the neighboring trees or rocks. Not one of their number, by this time, failed to know just where these shots had come from; and in a minute more, from all over the hillside below, thick and fast, the reports of the rifles were ringing on the morning air and the bullets came singing about the stone parapet, some of them chipping off little fragments from the top of the parapet itself, but most of them striking the great mass of rocks overhead and doing no harm whatever, except to spatter little fragments of lead upon the parapet and its gallant defenders.

"Watch for them! Keep your eyes peeled, Jim! Every time you see a head or an arm or a body coming from behind a rock or tree, let drive at it! It will give the idea that there are more of us up here than we really have, and we've got all the ammunition we can possibly use. Don't be afraid! I'll tell you when to save your cartridges. There's one now! Watch him!" Bang! went Pike's rifle. It was a good shot; for they could see that the bullet barked the tree just where the Apache was standing; but apparently it did no harm to the Indian himself; for the answering shot of his rifle was prompt, and the bullet whizzed dangerously near.

"That fellow's a cool hand!" said Pike. "Watch him, Jim, you're a little further that way. He'll be out again in a minute. What's the reason your man hasn't fired?—the man behind the rock that I told you to kill?"

"Because I'm certain that I hit him," said Jim, "and I reckon by this time he isn't doing any more shooting."

"Watch carefully, anyhow," was the reply. "They'll soon try, when they find there are very few of us, to crawl up the hill upon us. Then's the time you've got to note every movement! See! there comes one fellow behind that rock now. He's crawling on all fours. Thinks we can't see him. Now just hold on until he comes around that little ledge! —I'll take him! I've got him! Now!"

And again Pike's rifle rang out, and to his intense delight the Indian sprang to his feet—staggered an instant—and then fell all in a heap, huddled up around the roots of the tree which he was just striving to reach. Some one down among the Indians gave a yell of dismay. Evidently the one who was shot was a man of some prominence among them—possibly a chief.

"They'll try and haul his body out of the way, Jim. Watch for at least one or two of them coming up there! He may be only wounded, and they'll try to get him into safety. If they do—fire at the first man you see!"

Another minute, and then both the rifles blazed again. Two daring young Indians had made a rush forward, and had attempted to seize their wounded comrade; but the shots of the rifles whistling close about their ears, caused them to desist, to throw themselves on their faces, and then to roll or crawl away behind the adjacent rocks. Evidently they didn't care to expose themselves to the chance of further loss. Two Indians lying dead, and one over behind a rock possibly wounded, was enough to discourage even an Apache.

"They'll show again in a minute, though, Jim. Keep watch! They won't go away and leave those two bodies there if they can possibly help themselves. Some of them will stay. Of course, they'll have a consultation and then see if they can't get at us from the flank or from the rear. They can't; but they don't know it. That'll be their next game."

And so for the next five or ten minutes the siege was carried on, Jim and the old corporal watching the hillside, but meantime there was consternation back in the cave. Poor old Kate mingled moaning with prayers and tears; little Nellie, frightened, of course, as any child would be, lay sobbing with her head buried in Kate's lap. But Ned, brave little man that he was, had grasped his rifle, the Ballard, of which so much has already been said, and, crouching eagerly forward, before Pike knew it, the boy was close beside him at the stone wall, and had placed his hand upon his arm.

"Corporal, let me come in here beside you, there's room for

another. Do let me have one shot at them? Papa would if he were here, and I know it!"

This was altogether too much for Kate to bear. She dare not come forward, but from the dark recess in which she and Nellie were hidden, her cries and prayers broke forth again:

"For the love of all the saints, corporal, don't let that boy stay out there! Bring him back here to me! His father would kill me if anything happened to him! Oh, listen to me, Pike! Send the boy back again! Make him come!"

But so far from paying any attention to Kate's admonition, Pike turned with kindling eyes and patted the little fellow on the shoulder: "You're your father's own boy? Ned, and you shall stay here with me for the present at least, and if there should be a chance of a shot—one I can give you without exposing you—I'm going to let you have it. Kneel low down there, and don't lift your head above the parapet whatever you do! Stay just where you are."

With that the old trooper, whose rifle was still projecting through the loophole, again turned his attention to the Indians lurking among the rocks and bowlders down the hill. The two bodies still lay there—Jim's rifle covering them and threate-ning any Indians who might attempt to drag them away.

Every now and then, a black head would appear from behind some tree, but the instant it did so the darkey's rifle would ring out, the bullet would go whistling close beside it, the head would pop suddenly back, and Jim as promptly would re-load his rifle.

It was beginning to grow monotonous. The Indians— probably because they knew they were only wasting their scanty ammunition—had ceased firing, and were evidently calling to one another and signaling from behind the rocks and trees where they had taken refuge. So long as they remained down there in front Pike had no possible concern. His only fear, as has been said, was that they should make a combined rush. If they were to have sense enough to do that, and ignore the probability of losing three or four of their number in the attempt, it would be all over with the little party in the cave.

But the corporal had served too long among the Apaches to greatly dread any such move. They were already shaken by the severity of their reception and of their losses. He knew that they could not be aware that only two men and a little boy constituted the whole force of the defenders, for they would have come with a rush long before.

Their plan now would doubtless be to leave a few of their number in front to keep the besieged in check while the greater part of the band surrounded the big ledge and sought a means of getting at the little garrison from flank or rear.

What he hoped for was a chance of dealing them one more blow before they could crawl back out of range and presently the opportunity came. Two or three of the band who were farthest to the rear had managed to slip back some distance down the hill and occasional glimpses could now be caught of them as they stealthily made their way out towards the western slope. It was not long before their dirty white breech-clouts could be distinguished as they slowly and cautiously came creeping up hill.

"By George! Jim," muttered the old man with the ejaculation that with him supplied the place of trooper profanity—"I believe you're right about your Indian. You probably wounded him and he's lying behind that rock now, and those fellows are coming up to help him. Don't fire! They're too far away for a down-hill shot. Wait till I tell you. Now, Ned, my boy, run back and comfort Nellie a minute. I don't want you here where a glancing shot might hit you. The moment we get them started on the run, I'll call you."

Ned looked far from satisfied with the proposition, but the corporal was the commanding officer, and there was nothing to do but obey. He went reluctantly. "Mind, corporal, you've promised I should have a shot," he said, and Pike nodded assent, although he could not turn from his loophole. Another minute and the Henry rifle barked its loud challenge down the slope, and the old trooper's keen, set features relaxed in a grin.

"Now they've got two to lug," he muttered to Jim. "Lord! See that beggar roll over those rocks!"

Again there came yells and shots from down the hill but both were harmless. Cowed, apparently, by the sharp shooting of the defenders, the Apaches who had sought to rescue their wounded mate continued in hiding behind the rocks where they had taken shelter. The others, farther to the east, were slipping back as fast as they could, but studiously keeping out of sight of those death-dealing loopholes. Presently it was apparent to the corporal that a number of them had got together far down the hill and were holding excited controversy, probably as to the best means of getting possession of their dead friends and then, their living enemies. Pike looked at his watch. It was half after seven and they had been fighting an hour.

And now came a lull. Once in a long while some one of the besiegers would let drive a bullet at the loopholes, but Apache shooting was never of the best and though the lead spattered dangerously near, "the miss," quoth Pike, "is as good as any number of miles." On the other hand, whenever or wherever an Indian head, leg or arm appeared, it was instantly saluted by one, sometimes two, quick shots, and there could be no doubt whatever that the palefaces, as the Tontos supposed them all to be, were fully on the alert.

"Now, Jim, it won't be long before they will be showing around on all sides. Pile on a few more stones above that loophole that looks to the west. The next thing you know there'll be a head and a gun poked out from behind that shoulder of rock beyond you. I'll watch my side and keep a look on down the hill, too."

And now the hours seemed to drag with leaden weight. All was silence around them, yet Pike knew that this made their danger only the more imminent. He could nowhere see a sign of their late assailants except the stiffening bodies down the hill, but he had not a doubt that while some watched the front, most of them, making wide detours, were now lurking on every side, and looking for a possible opening. Every now and then he had to give a quick glance over his shoulder to see that Jim was alert and watchful. It would not do to have him fall asleep now. And then once in a while he listened, God only knows how wistfully, for the sound of cavalry coming across the westward plain. It surely was time for Sieber and the troops to be coming if the former had carried out his intentions. Pike could see nothing of the road towards Jarvis Pass and only a glimpse here and there of the plateau itself. The foliage in the larger trees was too thick. He longed to clamber to his watch-tower but felt well assured that one step outside the parapet would make him a target for the Indian rifles. First as an experiment he put his hat on a stick and cautiously raised it above their barricade. Two bullets instantly "zipped" over his head and dropped flat as pancakes from the rock overhead. The experiment was conclusive.

At last the straining ears of the watchers were attracted by strange sounds. Low calls in savage tongue from down the hill were answered on both sides and from above. The Indians had evidently thoroughly "reconnoitred" the position, and had found that there was actually no place around the rock from which they could see and open fire on the besieged. The sun was now high overhead. Odd sounds as of dragging objects began to be heard from the top of the rock, and this was kept up for fully an hour. Neither Pike nor Jim could imagine what it meant, but neither dared for an instant to leave his post.

It must have been eleven o'clock and after, when, all of a sudden, a black shadow rushed through the air, and Pike started almost to his feet as a huge log fell from above and bounded from the jagged rocks in front of them. Then came another, tumbling one upon the other, wedging and jostling, and speedily rising in a huge pile several feet high. More and more they came; then smaller ones; then loose dry branches and roots in quantities. And then, as the great heap grew and grew, an awful thought occurred to the old trooper. At first it seemed as though the Indians meant to try and form a "curtain," sheltered by which they could crawl upon their foes; but when the brushwood came, a fiercer, far more dreadful purpose was revealed. "My God!" he groaned, "they mean to roast us out."

CHAPTER X

LITTLE NED'S SHOT

From the babel of voices that reached old Pike's ears every now and then, and the bustle and noise going on overhead, he judged that there must be twenty or thirty Indians busily engaged in the work of heaping up firewood in front of the cave. The mountain side, as he well knew, was thickly strewn with dry branches, dead limbs, uprooted trees and all manner of combustible material, and the very warriors who, when around their own "rancheria," would have disdained doing a stroke of work of any kind, were now laboring like so many beavers to add to the great pile that was already almost on a level with the breastwork and not more than eight feet away. Some of the logs first thrown had rolled off and scattered down the slope, but enough had remained to make a sure foundation, and once this was accomplished the rest was easy work.

Poor Jim looked around imploringly at his superior.

"Ain't dey some way to stop that, corporal?" he asked.

"Don't you worry, Jim," was the prompt reply. "It will take them an hour more at least to get it big enough and then 'twill do no great harm. We can knock down our barricade so that they can't use it and fall back into the cave where it's dark and cool and where the smoke and flame can't reach us. Keep your eyes on your corner, man!" But though he spoke reassuringly, the old soldier felt a world of anxiety. Under cover of that huge heap of brushwood, growing bigger every minute, it would soon be possible for the Indians from below to crawl unseen close upon them, and set fire to the mass.

Even now he felt certain that there were several of the more daring of the Apaches lurking just around the corners which he and Jim were so faithfully guarding. The negro seemed so utterly abashed at his having been overcome by sleep during the hour before the dawn, and possibly so refreshed by that deep slumber, that now he was vigilance itself.

Within the cave old Kate had seen, of course, the falling of the logs and brushwood, and though she could not comprehend their object it served to keep in mind that their savage foes were all around her and her little charges, and to add to her alternate prayer and wailing. Unable to leave his post, Pike could only call sternly to her from time to time to cry shame upon her for frightening Nellie so, and to remind her that they had shot five Indians without getting a scratch themselves. "We can stand 'em off for hours yet, you old fool," he said, "and the boys from Verde are sure to get here to-day." And whether it was "old" or the "fool" in Pike's contemptuous remark, that stirred her resentment, it certainly resulted that Kate subsided into suffering and indignant protest. Then Ned's brave, boyish voice was heard.

"Corporal! Can't I come to you now? I'm no good here and I'm sick of the row Kate keeps up. You said you'd let me come back."

"Wait a few minutes, Ned. I want to be sure they are not sneaking around these corners," was the reply, followed almost instantly by the bang of Pike's carbine. Kate gave a suppressed shriek and the corporal a shout of exultation.

Encouraged by the sound of his voice to suppose that the guard on the east side of the barrier was neglecting his watch, a daring young Apache crawled on all fours around the foot of the rock to take an observation. The black head came in view even as Pike was speaking and the fierce eyes peered cautiously at the breastwork, but the corporal never moved a muscle, and the savage, believing himself unseen, crawled still further into view, until half his naked body was in sight from the narrow slit through which the old trooper was gazing. The brown muzzle of the cavalry carbine covered the creeping "brave," and the next instant the loud report went echoing over the gorge and the Indian, with one convulsive spring, fell back upon the ground writhing in the agonies of death. In striving to drag the body of his comrade back behind the rock another Tonto ventured to show head and shoulder, and came within an ace of sharing his fate, for Pike's next shot whistled within an inch of the flattened nose, and Apache number two dodged back with wonderful quickness, and did not again appear.

This would tend to keep them from sneaking around that particular corner, thought Pike, and he only wished that Jim could have similar luck on his side, but the Indians had grown wary. Time and again the veteran glanced down the hill to see if there was any sign of their crawling upon him from below, but that threatening pile of brushwood now hid most of the slope from his weary, anxious eyes. The crisis could not be long in coming.

"O God!" he prayed, "save these little children. Bring us aid."

Poor old Pike! Even as the whispered words fell from his lips a low, crackling sound caught his ear. Louder it grew, and, looking suddenly to the left, he saw a thin curl of smoke rising through the branches and gaining every instant in volume. Louder, louder snapped the blazing twigs. Denser, heavier grew the smoke. Then tiny darts of flame came shooting upward through the top of the pile and then yells of triumph and exultation rang from the rock above and the hillside below. A minute or two more, and while the Indians continued to pour fresh fuel from above, the great heap was a mass of roaring flame and the heat became intolerable. A puff of wind drove a huge volume of smoke and flame directly into Jim's nook in the fortification, and with a shout that he could hold on no longer the negro dropped back into the cave, rubbing his blinded eyes.

"Come back, Jim! Quick!" shouted Pike. "Down with these stones, now! Kick them over!—but watch for Indians on your side. Down with 'em!" and suiting action to the word the old soldier rolled rock after rock down towards the blazing pyre, until his side of the parapet was almost demolished. Half blinded by smoke and the scorching heat, he lost sight for a moment of the shoulder of the ledge on the east side. Two seconds more and it might have been all over with him, for now, relying on the fierce heat to drive the defenders back, a young Apache had stepped cautiously into view, caught sight of the tall old soldier pushing and kicking at the rocks, and, quick as a cat, up leaped the rifle to his shoulder. But quicker than any cat—quick as its own flash—there sounded the sudden crack of a target rifle, the Indian's gun flew up and was discharged in mid-air, while the owner, clapping his hand to his face, reeled back out of sight. The bullet of the little Ballard had taken him just under the eye, and as Pike turned in amazement at the double report, saw the Apache fall, and then turned to his left—there knelt little Ned, his blue eyes blazing, his boyish form quivering with excitement and triumph. Pike seized him in his arms and fairly kissed the glowing face. "God bless you, my boy! but you are a little soldier if there ever was one!" was his cry. "Now all three of us must watch the front. Keep as far forward as you can, Jim. We've got to hold those hounds back—until the boys come!"

Until the boys come! Heavens! When would that be? Here

was the day nearly half spent and no sign of relief for the little party battling so bravely for their lives at Sunset Pass. Where—where can the father be? Where is Al Sieber? Where the old comrades from Verde?

Let us see if we cannot find them, and then, with them, hasten to the rescue.

Far over near Jarvis Pass poor Captain Gwynne had been lying on the blankets the men eagerly spread for him, while the surgeon with Captain Turner's troops listened eagerly to the details of the night's work, and at the same time ministered to his exhausted patient. Turner, the other officers, and their favorite scout held brief and hurried consultation. It was decided to push at once for Sunset Pass; to leave Captain Gwynne here with most of his nearly worn-out escort; to mount the six Hualpai trailers they had with them on the six freshest horses, so as to get them to the scene of the tragedy as soon as possible, and then to start them afoot to follow the Apaches. In ten minutes Captain Turner, with Lieutenant Wilkins and forty troopers, was trotting off eastward following the lead of Sieber with his swarthy allies. Ten minutes more and Captain Gwynne had sufficiently revived to be made fully aware of what was going on, and was on his feet again in an instant. The surgeon vainly strove to detain him, but was almost rudely repulsed.

"Do you suppose I can rest one conscious minute until I know what has become of my babies?" he said. And climbing painfully into the saddle he clapped spurs to his horse and galloped after Turner's troop.

Finding it useless to argue, the doctor, with his orderly, mounted, too, and followed the procession. It was an hour before they came up with Turner's rearmost files and found burly Lieutenant Wilkins giving the men orders to keep well closed in case they had to increase the gait. The scouts and

Charles King

Sieber, far to the front, were galloping.

"What is it?" asked the doctor.

"Smoke," panted Wilkins. "The Hualpais saw it up the mountain south of the Pass."

Gwynne's haggard face was dreadful to see. The jar of the rough gallop had started afresh the bleeding in his head and the doctor begged him to wait and let him dress it again, but the only answer was a look of fierce determination, and renewed spurring of his wretched horse. He was soon abreast the head of the column, but even then kept on. Turner hailed him and urged him to stay with them, but entreaty was useless. "I am going after Sieber," was the answer. "Did you see the smoke?"

"No, Gwynne; but Sieber and the Hualpais are sure a big column went up and that it means the Apaches can't be far away. We're bound to get them. Don't wear yourself out, old fellow; stay with us!" but Gwynne pressed on. Far out to the front he could see that one of the Indian scouts had halted and was making signs. It took five minutes hard riding to reach him.

"What did you see? What has happened?" he gasped.

"Heap fire!" answered the Hualpai. "See?" But Gwynne's worn eyes could only make out the great mass of the mountain with its dark covering of stunted trees. He saw, however, that the scout was eagerly watching his comrades now so long a distance ahead. Presently the Indian shouted in excitement:

"Fight! Fight! Heap shoot, there!" and then at last the father's almost breaking heart regained a gleam of hope; a new light flashed in his eyes, new strength seemed to leap through his veins. Even his poor horse seemed to know that a supreme effort was needed and gamely answered the spur. Waving his hat above his head and shouting back to Turner "Come on!" the captain dashed away in pursuit of Sieber. Turner's men could hear no sound, but they saw the excitement in the signal; saw the sudden rush of Gwynne's steed, and nothing more was needed. "Gallop," rang the trumpet, and with carbines advanced and every eye on the dark gorge, still three miles before them, the riders of the beautiful "chestnut sorrel" troop swept across the plains.

Meantime the savage fight was going on and the defense was sorely pressed. Covered by the smoke caused by fresh armfuls of green wood hurled upon the fiery furnace in front of the cave, the vengeful Apaches had crawled to within a few yards of where the little breastwork had stood. Obedient to Pike's stern orders Kate had crept to the remotest corner of the recess and lay there flat upon the rock, holding Nellie in her arms. The corporal had bound a handkerchief about his left arm, for some of the besiegers, finding bullets of no avail, were firing Tonto arrows so that they fell into the mouth of the cave, and one of these had torn a deep gash midway between the elbow and the shoulder. Another had struck him on the thigh. Jim, too, had a bloody scratch. It stung and hurt and made him grit his teeth with rage and pain. Little Ned, sorely against his will, was screened by his father's saddle and some blankets, but he clung to his Ballard and the hope of at least one more shot.

And still, though sorely pressing the besieged, the Indians kept close under cover. The lessons of the morning had taught them that the pale faces could shoot fast and straight. They had lost heavily and could afford no more risks. But every moment their circle seemed closer to the mouth of the cave, and though direct assault could not now be made because of their great bonfire, the dread that weighed on Pike was that they should suddenly rush in from east and west. "In that event," said he to Jim, "we must sell our lives as dearly as possible. I'll have two at least before they can reach me."

Hardly had he spoken when bang came a shot from beyond the fire; a bullet zipped past his head and flattened on the rock well back in the cave. Where could that have come from? was the question. A little whiff of blue smoke sailing away on the wind from the fork of a tall oak not fifty feet in front told the story. Hidden from view of the besieged by the drifting smoke from the fire a young warrior had clambered until he reached the crotch and there had drawn up the rifle and belt tied by his comrades to a "lariat." Straddling a convenient branch and lashing himself to the trunk he was now in such a position that he could peer around the tree and aim right into the mouth of the rocky recess, and only one leg was exposed to the fire of the defense.

But that was one leg too much. "Blaze away at him, Jim," was the order. "We'll fire alternately." And Jim's bullet knocked a chip of bark into space, but did no further harm. "It's my turn now. Watch your side."

But before Pike could take aim there came a shot from the fork of the tree that well nigh robbed the little garrison of its brave leader. The corporal was just creeping forward to where he could rest his rifle on a little rock, and the Indian's bullet struck fairly in the shoulder, tore its way down along the muscles of the back, glanced upward from the shoulder blade, and, flattening on the rock overhead, fell almost before Ned's eyes. The shock knocked the old soldier flat on his face, and there came a yell of savage triumph from the tree, answered by yells from below and above. Ned, terror stricken, sprang to the old soldier's side, just as he was struggling to rise.

"Back! boy, back! They'll all be on us now. My God! Here they come! Now, Jim, fight for all you're worth."

Bang! bang! went the two rifles. Bang! bang! bang! came the shots from both sides and from the front, while the dusky forms could be seen creeping up the rocks east and west of the fire, yelling like fiends. Crack! went Ned's little Ballard again, and Pike seized the boy and fairly thrust him into the depths of the cave. A lithe, naked form leaped into sight just at the entrance and then went crashing down into the blazing embers below. Another Indian gone. Bang! bang! bang! Heavier came the uproar of the shots below. Bang! bang! "Good God!" groaned Pike. "Has the whole Apache nation come to reinforce them? Yell, you hounds—aye—yell! There are only two of us!" Shots came ringing thick and fast. Yells resounded along the mountain side, but they seemed more of warning than of hatred and defiance. Bang! bang! bang! the rifles rattled up the rocky slopes, but where could the bullets go? Not one had struck in the cave for fully ten seconds, yet the rattle and roar of musketry seemed redoubled. What can it mean? Pike creeps still further forward to get a shot at the first Indian that shows himself, but pain and weakness are dimming the sight of his keen, brave eyes; perhaps telling on his hearing. Listen, man! Listen! Those are not Indian yells now resounding down the rocks. Listen, Pike, old friend, old soldier, old hero! Too late—too late! Just as a ringing trumpet call, "Cease firing," comes thrilling up the steep, and little Ned once more leaps forward to aid him, the veteran falls upon his face and all is darkness.

Another moment, and now the very hillside seems to burst into shouts and cheers,—joy, triumph, infinite relief. Victory shines on face after face as the bronzed troopers come crowding to the mouth of the cave. Tenderly they raise Pike from the ground and bear him out into the sunshine. Respectfully they make way for Captain Turner as he springs into their midst and clasps little Nellie in his arms; and poor old Kate, laughing, weeping and showering blessings on "the boys," is frantically shaking hands with man after man. So, too, is Black Jim. And then, half carried, half led, by two stalwart soldiers, Captain Gwynne is borne, trembling like an aspen, into their midst, and, kneeling on the rocky floor, clasps his little ones to his breast, and the strong man sobs aloud his thanks to God for their wonderful preservation.

*   *   *   *   *

"Papa—papa, I shot an Indian!" How many a time little Ned has to shout it, in his eager young voice, before the father can realize what is being said.

"It's the truth he's telling, sir," said a big sergeant. "There's wan of 'em lies at the corner there with a hole no bigger than a *pay* under the right eye," and the captain knows not what to say. The surgeon's stimulants have restored Pike to conscious-ness, and Gwynne kneels again to take the old soldier's hands in his. Dry eyes are few. Hearts are all too full for many words. After infinite peril and suffering, after most gallant defense, after a night of terror and a day of fiercest battle, the little party was rescued, one and all, to life and love and such a welcome when at last they were brought back to Verde, where Pike was nursed back to strength and health, where Nellie was caressed as a heroine, and where little Ned was petted and well nigh spoiled as "the boy that shot an Indian"—and if he did brag about it occasionally, when he came east to school, who can blame him? But when they came they did not this time try the route of Sunset Pass.

THE END

Choose from Thousands of 1stWorldLibrary Classics By

A. M. Barnard
Ada Leverson
Adolphus William Ward
Aesop
Agatha Christie
Alexander Aaronsohn
Alexander Kielland
Alexandre Dumas
Alfred Gatty
Alfred Ollivant
Alice Duer Miller
Alice Turner Curtis
Alice Dunbar
Allen Chapman
Alleyne Ireland
Ambrose Bierce
Amelia E. Barr
Amory H. Bradford
Andrew Lang
Andrew McFarland Davis
Andy Adams
Angela Brazil
Anna Alice Chapin
Anna Sewell
Annie Besant
Annie Hamilton Donnell
Annie Payson Call
Annie Roe Carr
Annonaymous
Anton Chekhov
Archibald Lee Fletcher
Arnold Bennett
Arthur C. Benson
Arthur Conan Doyle
Arthur M. Winfield
Arthur Ransome
Arthur Schnitzler
Arthur Train
Atticus
B.H. Baden-Powell
B. M. Bower
B. C. Chatterjee
Baroness Emmuska Orczy
Baroness Orczy
Basil King
Bayard Taylor
Ben Macomber
Bertha Muzzy Bower
Bjornstjerne Bjornson

Booth Tarkington
Boyd Cable
Bram Stoker
C. Collodi
C. E. Orr
C. M. Ingleby
Carolyn Wells
Catherine Parr Traill
Charles A. Eastman
Charles Amory Beach
Charles Dickens
Charles Dudley Warner
Charles Farrar Browne
Charles Ives
Charles Kingsley
Charles Klein
Charles Hanson Towne
Charles Lathrop Pack
Charles Romyn Dake
Charles Whibley
Charles Willing Beale
Charlotte M. Braeme
Charlotte M. Yonge
Charlotte Perkins Stetson
Clair W. Hayes
Clarence Day Jr.
Clarence E. Mulford
Clemence Housman
Confucius
Coningsby Dawson
Cornelis DeWitt Wilcox
Cyril Burleigh
D. H. Lawrence
Daniel Defoe
David Garnett
Dinah Craik
Don Carlos Janes
Donald Keyhoe
Dorothy Kilner
Dougan Clark
Douglas Fairbanks
E. Nesbit
E. P. Roe
E. Phillips Oppenheim
E. S. Brooks
Earl Barnes
Edgar Rice Burroughs
Edith Van Dyne
Edith Wharton

Edward Everett Hale
Edward J. O'Biren
Edward S. Ellis
Edwin L. Arnold
Eleanor Atkins
Eleanor Hallowell Abbott
Eliot Gregory
Elizabeth Gaskell
Elizabeth McCracken
Elizabeth Von Arnim
Ellem Key
Emerson Hough
Emilie F. Carlen
Emily Bronte
Emily Dickinson
Enid Bagnold
Enilor Macartney Lane
Erasmus W. Jones
Ernie Howard Pie
Ethel May Dell
Ethel Turner
Ethel Watts Mumford
Eugene Sue
Eugenie Foa
Eugene Wood
Eustace Hale Ball
Evelyn Everett-green
Everard Cotes
F. H. Cheley
F. J. Cross
F. Marion Crawford
Fannie E. Newberry
Federick Austin Ogg
Ferdinand Ossendowski
Fergus Hume
Florence A. Kilpatrick
Fremont B. Deering
Francis Bacon
Francis Darwin
Frances Hodgson Burnett
Frances Parkinson Keyes
Frank Gee Patchin
Frank Harris
Frank Jewett Mather
Frank L. Packard
Frank V. Webster
Frederic Stewart Isham
Frederick Trevor Hill
Frederick Winslow Taylor

Friedrich Kerst
Friedrich Nietzsche
Fyodor Dostoyevsky
G.A. Henty
G.K. Chesterton
Gabrielle E. Jackson
Garrett P. Serviss
Gaston Leroux
George A. Warren
George Ade
Geroge Bernard Shaw
George Cary Eggleston
George Durston
George Ebers
George Eliot
George Gissing
George MacDonald
George Meredith
George Orwell
George Sylvester Viereck
George Tucker
George W. Cable
George Wharton James
Gertrude Atherton
Gordon Casserly
Grace E. King
Grace Gallatin
Grace Greenwood
Grant Allen
Guillermo A. Sherwell
Gulielma Zollinger
Gustav Flaubert
H. A. Cody
H. B. Irving
H.C. Bailey
H. G. Wells
H. H. Munro
H. Irving Hancock
H. R. Naylor
H. Rider Haggard
H. W. C. Davis
Haldeman Julius
Hall Caine
Hamilton Wright Mabie
Hans Christian Andersen
Harold Avery
Harold McGrath
Harriet Beecher Stowe
Harry Castlemon
Harry Coghill
Harry Houidini

Hayden Carruth
Helent Hunt Jackson
Helen Nicolay
Hendrik Conscience
Hendy David Thoreau
Henri Barbusse
Henrik Ibsen
Henry Adams
Henry Ford
Henry Frost
Henry James
Henry Jones Ford
Henry Seton Merriman
Henry W Longfellow
Herbert A. Giles
Herbert Carter
Herbert N. Casson
Herman Hesse
Hildegard G. Frey
Homer
Honore De Balzac
Horace B. Day
Horace Walpole
Horatio Alger Jr.
Howard Pyle
Howard R. Garis
Hugh Lofting
Hugh Walpole
Humphry Ward
Ian Maclaren
Inez Haynes Gillmore
Irving Bacheller
Isabel Cecilia Williams
Isabel Hornibrook
Israel Abrahams
Ivan Turgenev
J.G.Austin
J. Henri Fabre
J. M. Barrie
J. M. Walsh
J. Macdonald Oxley
J. R. Miller
J. S. Fletcher
J. S. Knowles
J. Storer Clouston
J. W. Duffield
Jack London
Jacob Abbott
James Allen
James Andrews
James Baldwin

James Branch Cabell
James DeMille
James Joyce
James Lane Allen
James Lane Allen
James Oliver Curwood
James Oppenheim
James Otis
James R. Driscoll
Jane Abbott
Jane Austen
Jane L. Stewart
Janet Aldridge
Jens Peter Jacobsen
Jerome K. Jerome
Jessie Graham Flower
John Buchan
John Burroughs
John Cournos
John F. Kennedy
John Gay
John Glasworthy
John Habberton
John Joy Bell
John Kendrick Bangs
John Milton
John Philip Sousa
John Taintor Foote
Jonas Lauritz Idemil Lie
Jonathan Swift
Joseph A. Altsheler
Joseph Carey
Joseph Conrad
Joseph E. Badger Jr
Joseph Hergesheimer
Joseph Jacobs
Jules Vernes
Julian Hawthrone
Julie A Lippmann
Justin Huntly McCarthy
Kakuzo Okakura
Karle Wilson Baker
Kate Chopin
Kenneth Grahame
Kenneth McGaffey
Kate Langley Bosher
Kate Langley Bosher
Katherine Cecil Thurston
Katherine Stokes
L. A. Abbot
L. T. Meade

L. Frank Baum
Latta Griswold
Laura Dent Crane
Laura Lee Hope
Laurence Housman
Lawrence Beasley
Leo Tolstoy
Leonid Andreyev
Lewis Carroll
Lewis Sperry Chafer
Lilian Bell
Lloyd Osbourne
Louis Hughes
Louis Joseph Vance
Louis Tracy
Louisa May Alcott
Lucy Fitch Perkins
Lucy Maud Montgomery
Luther Benson
Lydia Miller Middleton
Lyndon Orr
M. Corvus
M. H. Adams
Margaret E. Sangster
Margret Howth
Margaret Vandercook
Margaret W. Hungerford
Margret Penrose
Maria Edgeworth
Maria Thompson Daviess
Mariano Azuela
Marion Polk Angellotti
Mark Overton
Mark Twain
Mary Austin
Mary Catherine Crowley
Mary Cole
Mary Hastings Bradley
Mary Roberts Rinehart
Mary Rowlandson
M. Wollstonecraft Shelley
Maud Lindsay
Max Beerbohm
Myra Kelly
Nathaniel Hawthrone
Nicolo Machiavelli
O. F. Walton
Oscar Wilde
Owen Johnson
P.G. Wodehouse
Paul and Mabel Thorne

Paul G. Tomlinson
Paul Severing
Percy Brebner
Percy Keese Fitzhugh
Peter B. Kyne
Plato
Quincy Allen
R. Derby Holmes
R. L. Stevenson
R. S. Ball
Rabindranath Tagore
Rahul Alvares
Ralph Bonehill
Ralph Henry Barbour
Ralph Victor
Ralph Waldo Emmerson
Rene Descartes
Ray Cummings
Rex Beach
Rex E. Beach
Richard Harding Davis
Richard Jefferies
Richard Le Gallienne
Robert Barr
Robert Frost
Robert Gordon Anderson
Robert L. Drake
Robert Lansing
Robert Lynd
Robert Michael Ballantyne
Robert W. Chambers
Rosa Nouchette Carey
Rudyard Kipling
Saint Augustine
Samuel B. Allison
Samuel Hopkins Adams
Sarah Bernhardt
Sarah C. Hallowell
Selma Lagerlof
Sherwood Anderson
Sigmund Freud
Standish O'Grady
Stanley Weyman
Stella Benson
Stella M. Francis
Stephen Crane
Stewart Edward White
Stijn Streuvels
Swami Abhedananda
Swami Parmananda
T. S. Ackland

T. S. Arthur
The Princess Der Ling
Thomas A. Janvier
Thomas A Kempis
Thomas Anderton
Thomas Bailey Aldrich
Thomas Bulfinch
Thomas De Quincey
Thomas Dixon
Thomas H. Huxley
Thomas Hardy
Thomas More
Thornton W. Burgess
U. S. Grant
Upton Sinclair
Valentine Williams
Various Authors
Vaughan Kester
Victor Appleton
Victor G. Durham
Victoria Cross
Virginia Woolf
Wadsworth Camp
Walter Camp
Walter Scott
Washington Irving
Wilbur Lawton
Wilkie Collins
Willa Cather
Willard F. Baker
William Dean Howells
William le Queux
W. Makepeace Thackeray
William W. Walter
William Shakespeare
Winston Churchill
Yei Theodora Ozaki
Yogi Ramacharaka
Young E. Allison
Zane Grey

.

www.ingramcontent.com/pod-product-compliance
Lightning Source LLC
Chambersburg PA
CBHW031852170626
46807CB00004B/1683